"I don't see you walking away," he commented.

"I'm thinking about it!" I snapped.

"But you're not doing it."

"Is that a dare?"

He chuckled and pulled me closer to him. I felt his lips on top of my head, and his warm breath.

"You never refuse a dare, do you, Tobey?" His voice sounded low and different somehow.

"Never!"

"And what if I dared you to kiss me?"

I swallowed hard. "You wouldn't!" I said in a small voice.

"Is that what you really think?"

Dear Readers,

We at Silhouette would like to thank all our readers for your many enthusiastic letters. In direct response to your encouragement, we are now publishing *four* FIRST LOVEs every month.

As always FIRST LOVEs are written especially for and about you—your hopes, your dreams, your ambitions.

Please continue to share your suggestions and comments with us; they play an important part in our pleasing you.

I invite you to write to us at the address below:

Nancy Jackson
Senior Editor
Silhouette Books
P.O. Box 769
New York, N.Y. 10019

A PASSING GAME
Beverly Sommers

First Love from Silhouette

Published by Silhouette Books New York

America's Publisher of Contemporary Romance

Other First Loves by Beverly Sommers

Up to Date

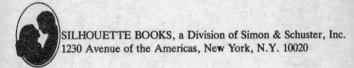

SILHOUETTE BOOKS, a Division of Simon & Schuster, Inc.
1230 Avenue of the Americas, New York, N.Y. 10020

Copyright © 1983 by Beverly Sommers

Distributed by Pocket Books

ISBN: 0-671-53374-6

First Silhouette Books printing December, 1983

10 9 8 7 6 5 4 3 2 1

America's Publisher of Contemporary Romance

Printed in the U.S.A.

A PASSING GAME

1

I have hair the exact same color as potato chips—
the regular kind, not the barbeque. This doesn't
really have to do with anything—it's just that
someone noticed that about my hair the other day
and it kind of stuck in my mind, so I thought I'd
mention it.

My hair is not my best feature. Maybe it's my
second best or even my third, but then again maybe
it isn't. I've noticed that people are very often
wrong about what they think their very best feature
is and sometimes pick something that makes you
stare at them in amazement. So anyway, I don't
know about my hair, but I do know absolutely what
my best feature is and that is my foot. To be more
exact, my right foot.

I have the strongest right foot of anyone I know. Maybe even of anyone in the world, but I don't know that for a fact. This condition is partly thanks to my mom, who made me take ballet dancing for years and years. Even though I was about as graceful as a cow and absolutely detested having to dress in leotards and a tutu, I have to credit ballet lessons for making my foot as strong as it is today.

My foot is my secret weapon, although it's not going to be a secret for much longer. I don't mean that it's a lethal weapon—I don't go in for karate or anything weird like that. What my foot is good for, absolutely perfect for, is kicking a football.

I've known this about my foot as far back as the sixth grade, but it was something I hadn't done anything major about all through my first year of high school. In the sixth grade the boys were still willing to play football with the girls, and I was always their favorite because I was the only one who could kick extra points over the designated branch of a tree. I also could punt very well. I don't throw badly either, but I don't delude myself into thinking that anyone is going to let me be a quarterback. We girls might have come a long way, but we're not that far yet, and anyway, all the boys always want to be quarterback and most of *them* don't even get to be it.

In junior high, the only boys who would let the girls play football with them were the kind who got some kind of cheap thrill out of tackling a girl's body. I defected from team play at that point and began practicing on my own. I generally put in maybe two hours a day on my kicking, more during school vacations. My little sister, Robin, aided me in this, holding the ball for me while I practiced place kicks. Admittedly, she did this not out of any altruistic motive or for love of her big sister; she did it because I threatened to punch her out if she refused.

Now that the iron was hot, or rather the foot, I was ready to strike. I should have done it last year when I was a freshman, but I chickened out at the last minute. At the beginning of last year I confided to my best friend, Charles, what I intended to do. He scratched his head, looked very, very serious, and then said, "Don't. Do not under any circumstances even consider it. Don't even think about it. Cease. Desist. You are courting disaster." Charles always repeats himself in case someone doesn't understand him the first time.

Since Charles is always right, I took his advice. And later I was very sorry. Our school football team last year didn't make one field goal or one extra point. With me on the team they could have turned a losing season into a winning one, but they didn't even know what they had missed out on. This year I was going to give them a chance to find out.

It was now one week before school starts, and the varsity team was already working out. I knew this because Charles and I rode our bikes past the football field every day on our way to the beach.

Neither of us goes to the beach to get a tan. I go because I've heard running in the sand strengthens the feet; Charles goes because he fancies himself an amateur marine biologist, even though it's only Lake Michigan we're talking about, not one of the oceans. Charles collects specimens of things and then takes them home and looks at them under his microscope. Sometimes I look at them, but they all look the same to me.

You are probably wondering why a fifteen-year-old girl would have a boy for a best friend. I know my mother wonders about it all the time. The main reason is that Charles lives right across the street from me and we've known each other all our lives. When we were little kids, none of the boys in the neighborhood ever wanted to play with Charles, because he wasn't interested in sports and that's all they were interested in. They called him a sissy. He *is* a sissy, but he's an interesting one.

At the same time, I refused to play with any of the little girls that lived nearby, because all they wanted to play was dolls or house or dress-up. Jump rope? Forget it!

So Charles and I sort of gravitated toward each other, and I've always found him to be a most satisfactory friend. There is just this one major difference between us: Charles is the most noncompetitive person I know, while I, on the other hand, am super competitive. We don't compete with each other, though, because our friendship is on a strictly intellectual level. Charles is also very understanding. Through the years, whenever I've deserted him to play football or baseball or basketball with the boys, he has always understood and forgiven me. I, on the other hand, always understand and forgive him when he gets better grades than I do. This is an area where I don't feel competitive, as that would necessitate studying harder.

After reconnoitering the football field with Charles for four full days, stopping on our bikes briefly to watch the players trying out for the different positions under Coach McKeever's direction, while elsewhere on the field his assistant coaches were putting the players through drills, I felt my own audition could no longer be put off and picked Friday to be the day. It was, oddly enough, a Friday the 13th, but I figured that day would only prove unlucky to the boy whose job I was about to walk away with.

On the appointed day, I announced to my sister, Robin, at breakfast that I was going to take her to the beach. The announcement seemed to have the same effect as if a celestial voice had declared the end of the world. Three pairs of eyes turned in my direction. Three mouths hung open, displaying various foods within. I might add that I had never before offered to take Robin anywhere, but still I hadn't expected such a strong reaction.

"Why?" asked Robin, when she could finally manage to speak. My parents' eyes mirrored her question.

Rather than come up with a good reason, I went on the offensive. "Don't you want to go?"

"I want to, Tobey, I want to. I'll be ready in five minutes, I promise," she said, knocking over her glass of milk in her excitement.

"Finish your breakfast first," my mother began, but Robin was already out of the room. I sat back to enjoy my own repast. Being in training, I always insist on a big breakfast.

"That was nice of you, honey," said my father. "You girls should be better friends."

"She's only ten," I reminded him, feeling a slight bit guilty that my motives were definitely ulterior.

It's not that I mind Robin. As little sisters go, she's all right, but the interests of a ten-year-old and a fifteen-year-old do not exactly coincide. I was there for her when she needed me, like on matters of advice, but socially we went our separate ways. She was, however, very good at holding the football while I kicked. She had to be; I had trained her.

I was already dressed in running shorts and t-shirt over my bikini. After breakfast I went upstairs to my room, threw Grogan the cat off my bed, and made it up quickly. Grogan was just as quick and was back on it before I had pulled the bedspread over the pillow. Grogan is supposed to be my mother's cat, but for some reason he seems to prefer my bed to sleep on.

I put on some cotton socks and my best pair of broken-in running shoes. I made two pigtails out of my hair with rubber bands, trying not to get my hair caught up in them. Mother says they break off the hair, but all I care about is that they keep it off my face. I wet my bangs to plaster them down, but I knew the humidity would soon fluff them up. I have the kind of hair that changes with the weather. Dad always says he knows when it's going to rain just by looking at me. Some people's hair droops in the rain; mine curls up.

I usually just take a towel with me to the beach, but this time I got my zippered canvas bag out of the closet and put my football in the bottom, covering it with a beach towel. When I got back downstairs, Robin was already waiting outside. She had both our bikes out of the garage and ready.

"Stay right behind me, Robin," I cautioned her.

"I know how to ride a bike, Tobey!" Of course she did. I was beginning to sound like my mother. Anyone at ten knows how to ride a bike.

"Just one thing," I told her as we coasted down our driveway, "I want to make a stop on the way to the beach."

"We stopping for food?"

"No, not for food."

"Where are we stopping?"

"At the high school."

There was a silence behind me, then, "Why do we have to stop there?"

"It's right on the way, Robin."

"Yeah, but why do we have to stop?" Ten-year-olds invariably ask too many questions.

13

I took a deep breath. My secret was about to be told. "I want to try out for the football team."

I could hear her giggling. "I'm serious, Robin, and I don't want to hear you laughing. It might just undermine my confidence."

The giggling stopped. "Girls don't play football, Tobey."

"Who told you that?"

"Everyone knows that. I mean, I know you can kick the ball and all that, but they're not going to let you on the team."

She's pretty sharp for ten. "That was in the old days, Robin; times have changed. Legally they can't prevent me from trying out."

"Are you sure?"

I wasn't, actually, but I just didn't see how stopping me could be legal. I had heard of a couple of cases of girls playing on varsity basketball teams, so I didn't see why football would be any different. I supposed there were no girls playing football because there weren't any girls who played that well. I was soon to be the exception, I told myself.

"Trust me," I told her, and we rode the rest of the way in silence. I'm sure she *did* trust me. Robin is a very trusting girl, and everything I say to her she takes as the absolute truth and final authority, which means that I can't tell her things lightly. For some reason she believes me to be the font of all knowledge. She will even take my word on a subject over that of my parents. This is a heavy responsibility, but one that I gladly assume.

Robin, through some quirk of fortune, does not have hair the color of potato chips. She has dark brown, straight, silky hair of the type that runs in my family. I am the anomaly, but when I become an adult, I plan on having mine straightened and dyed that exact same color—unless, of course, I change my mind in the interim.

When we reached the high school, I rode by the football field, continuing until we got to the bike racks in the parking lot. We locked our bikes and, me carrying my canvas bag, casually took a stroll over to the area where practice was going on.

I had no intention of marching right up to Coach McKeever and telling him I wanted to try out. I thought that first I would have Robin hold the ball for me while I made a few practice kicks. I was sure that when he saw how high and far I could kick, I wouldn't have to go to him. He would come to me.

I am aware I'm sounding very conceited over my kicking prowess, but that's because I really am very good at kicking. There is an almost endless list of things I do not do at all well, and I'll be the first to admit it in each case. In fact, the only thing that I really do well is kick a football, and that's the result of hundreds of hours of hard practice. It's just a fact of life about me, that's all. I have hair the color of potato chips. I can kick a football well. That's it—two truths about me. Anything else is open to debate, but not those two facts.

I could see that Robin was nervous about being the only little kid on the field and one of the only two girls. I knew I'd have to reassure her if I wanted her to hold the ball well for me.

"I guess I could have gotten one of the boys to hold the ball for me, Robin, but it wouldn't have been the same. You're the best person at holding a ball that I've ever seen."

"Am I really, Tobey?"

"Didn't I just say you were?"

She nodded, blushing over the compliment.

I took my football out of the bag and positioned Robin with it several yards from where the practice was going on. I could see that several of the boys were looking in our direction, and I was hoping they'd keep on looking while I gave my demonstration. The coach was not looking in our direction, but I was confident that would soon change.

When Robin got the ball positioned to my satisfaction, I got several feet behind it, crossed my fingers, and began to run towards the ball. My toe connected with the pigskin, and I got off one of my better kicks. We were parallel to the football field, and I kicked at about the 20-yard line. I watched as the ball soared through the air, not dropping until it reached about the 30-yard line at the other end of the field. An impressive kick, if I do say so myself.

Without even deigning to glance over to see what the reaction was, I took Robin in tow and we trotted down the sidelines to retrieve the football. What I had in mind was sending another place kick back, and then getting off a few punts. My place kicks are good, but my punts are awesome.

My return kick was equally impressive. I wished I could have kicked out on the field for a try at getting the ball over the uprights. I left Robin to stay where she was, so that I could punt to her, and trotted back down the field to get my ball. A surreptitious glance told me that an audience was now gathered to watch me.

I picked up the ball, took a couple of steps and punted it down to Robin. She misjudged it—it went sailing over her head. I rested, hands on my hips, as she went charging after it. It was at that point that I noticed a couple of the boys heading in my direction. I pretended that I didn't notice them until they were right next to me. Then I saw that one of them was Billy Rafferty, a bully who lives down the street from me. When he was younger he used to beat up little kids; now he went in for verbal abuse, with the worst mouth of any boy in school.

"What do you think you're trying to prove, Tobey?" he asked me in his nasty way.

"You have nothing to worry about, Billy. I'm not trying out for tackle."

His friend sniggered at this remark, which got Billy a little hot under the collar. "You're not trying out for anything—you think we want a *girl* on the team?"

The way he said *girl* made it sound like an undesirable subspecies. Typical of Billy, one of the most ignorant boys I know.

"When did they make you the coach?" I asked

him. By now several more of the players had gathered around, and they were all laughing. Billy can't stand being laughed at.

"Why don't you and your little sister go home and play dolls," he said with a sneer.

"Gonna join us with your Kenny doll?" I asked him sweetly, and if looks could kill, I'd have been dead at that moment. The truth of the matter is Billy had once owned a Kenny doll when he was about eight, which I'm sure he hadn't forgotten. I was even more sure he wouldn't want his buddies to find out.

He started to say something else, then thought better of it and just stood there scowling.

I saw that Robin had returned with the ball, but by this time I was surrounded by most of the team, so she stood shyly at a distance. Then the boys moved apart, and I saw that I had at last gotten the coach's attention.

I had Coach McKeever for civics freshman year, and he knew who I was because I had, on several occasions, started discussions in his class. Well, arguments really.

"Hi, Tobey, did you come to join the team?" He asked it in a joking manner, so I had to assume he hadn't seen my kicks.

"That's right, coach," I told him, not caring at all that the boys were now all laughing. "My school spirit impels me to rescue you from another losing season."

I could see he was torn between ordering me off

the field and being diplomatic to one of his students. I had always gotten the feeling he liked me in class, because whenever the subject began to get boring and the kids started falling asleep, I would always come up with something that would provoke an argument. Not all teachers like this, of course, but civics had been one of my more successful classes.

"What position did you have in mind?" His tone was a little condescending, but I wasn't going to let that put me off.

"Just kicker, coach," I said modestly. "I don't pretend to be big enough for anything else."

He was standing there with his arms crossed, chewing on his lip. I think he was looking at me, but I couldn't be positive, because he was wearing sunglasses. "You know, Tobey, it might not be a bad idea if you tried to organize a girls' football team. I bet you could get a lot of girls interested."

I'd be willing to bet I couldn't even get *one* girl interested, but I didn't say so.

"You need a kicker, coach, and I'm a good kicker."

He spread out his arms. "Look, Tobey—"

"Aren't girls allowed to try out for the team? Is there some rule against it?" If there was, I wanted to hear about it right away.

He shook his head. "No, there's no rule."

"Then I want to try out."

Wynn Neil, the most popular boy in school by virtue of being the starting quarterback and having dark, curly hair and almost a mustache, stepped up to the coach's side. "Why don't you give her a try, coach? I wouldn't mind being able to count on a few field goals this season. With a good kicker, we might make it to the playoffs."

I knew that, being the star of the team, he could afford to say something like that. Nothing I might do would be at all threatening to him; his position was assured. I flashed him my most dazzling smile and saw an answering gleam in his dark eyes.

Some of the boys immediately took his side. Others, probably potential kickers, began to grumble. Billy, who had nothing to worry about, was grumbling the loudest of all. I knew he had had it in for me ever since I beat him once at arm wrestling. In those days, though, he had been much smaller. Now his arms were about the size of my legs!

One of McKeever's assistant coaches and probably the youngest teacher in the school, Mr. Melville, suddenly took up my cause. "I'd like to see what the kid can do, Mac. God knows we could use a kicker on the team."

The coach made his first decisive move. He lifted up the whistle that was resting on his chest, blew it, and ordered the team back to the field. I could see they obeyed him with reluctance. Then he looked at me. "Okay, come along and show me what you can do. Who's the little girl over there?"

"That's my sister—she holds the ball for me."

"One of the boys can hold it for you."

Oh, no—no way! One of the guys might just let it go too soon and purposefully foul up my kick. "I'd rather use Robin."

"Yeah, okay, but get this straight. *She's* not trying out for the team."

"She's not even in high school yet," I said, getting in the last word.

The boys were supposed to be resuming their practice, but I could see they were all watching to see how I'd do.

"What's your field goal range?" the coach asked me.

"I don't know. I haven't ever practiced on a real field," I admitted to him. I could see he looked doubtful.

"Well, we'll try it from the thirty," he said, leading Robin out onto the field and telling her where to position herself.

I could see that Robin was nervous, but I figured she was too afraid of me to goof up. I was nervous, too, but also exhilarated. This was my big chance, and I didn't want to blow it.

With the coach standing skeptically on the sidelines, I backed up a few yards, then began to run. I got off a good kick and, for the first time in my life, saw it go through the uprights instead of through the branches of a tree. I felt I was up in the air right along with the ball, willing it over by the strength of my mind.

I saw Robin jumping up and down in excitement, and I looked over at the coach. He wasn't jumping up and down in excitement, but he wasn't looking doubtful anymore, either.

"Was that a fluke or can you do it again?" he asked me.

"I can do it again."

"Let's see it."

I did it six more times before he finally believed me. Then he asked me if I could punt.

"Sure I can punt," I told him, feeling pretty cocky by that time.

Robin ran over and stood by the coach while he threw out footballs to me, and I punted each one. After several punts, I think he got the message.

Mr. Melville came over and put his arm around my shoulders, then yelled over to the coach. "You've got to use her, Mac. There'll be nothing stopping us with a kicker on the team. Good lord, man—she's the answer to our prayers!"

My fantasy was coming true, easier and even better than I had fantasized it. I was going to step right in and save the season for Evanston High.

Coach McKeever motioned me over to him. "You looked good, Tobey, I gotta admit it. I guess if you really want the position, it's yours."

I wanted to jump in the air and scream, do an Indian war dance, shout to the skies. Instead, I maintained my cool. "I want it, coach."

He looked over at Mr. Melville. "I don't know how the team's going to take this."

"They'll take it all right when we start winning," said Mr. Melville.

"If it would make things easier for you," I said, "I can practice at home. I do every day anyway."

The coach shook his head. "No, you're part of the team now, and you'll practice with them. Go on inside and get fitted with a uniform."

I looked at Robin standing so patiently waiting for me. "I promised to take my little sister to the beach. Couldn't I wait until Monday?"

"Okay, Tobey, but I expect to see you out here after school on Monday—and every day thereafter."

I wanted to throw myself in his arms and hug him, but instead I held out my hand. He looked surprised, then held out his own and we shook on it.

"Thanks, coach, you won't regret this," I told him.

As I was turning away, I heard Mr. Melville say, "Isn't that a line from some movie?"

It was, but I had been hoping I was the only one who watched old movies on television. Of course they were both so old they probably weren't old movies to them.

I was leaving the field with Robin when Wynn Neil hailed me from another part of the field. I turned in his direction and shaded my eyes to see him.

"Did you make it?" he shouted, and I could see the other boys in the area waiting for my answer.

I held up my arm and flashed him a V with my fingers.

23

"Way to go," he yelled. I was really pleased to hear his response. If I had the quarterback on my side, I really wasn't worried about the rest of the team. In fact, I wasn't worried about anything at all at that moment. I think I can truthfully say it was the happiest moment of my life up until then, and I was savoring every bit of it.

2

My euphoria extended over to Robin, to whom I was munificent the remainder of the day. I let her stay at the beach as long as she wanted, bought her everything to eat that her little heart desired and even allowed her to ride my ten-speed bike home while I rode on her three-speed.

I took her to one of the beaches not frequented by the high school crowd. Luckily some of Robin's friends were there, so I didn't need to be constantly entertaining her. While she and some of her friends swam out to the float, I spread out my towel and relaxed in the sun. I was wishing I had Charles there to talk to and could hardly wait to get home in order to tell him about my triumph. That it was a triumph, I had no doubts. Oh, I knew I was a good kicker, and I further knew the team needed me, but I hadn't really envisioned being given a place on the team that easily.

The really difficult part would be to get the other players to accept me, but this didn't really bother me. I was getting my chance to play on the team, which is all I really wanted. If they chose to be churlish and give me a hard time, that was their problem, not mine. I knew Billy would give me a hard time, but unless his family decided to give him a lobotomy at some point, Billy would always be giving someone a hard time. That was just Billy's nature. At least Wynn Neil had been friendly, and if I had the support of the most popular boy in school, that wasn't so bad.

I took Robin to Burger King for lunch, and over our Whoppers and fries she said to me, "Gee, Tobey, you'll get to know all the boys on the football team."

Robin is rather astute for ten.

"I'm not interested in boys, Robin."

"Why not?"

"Because they're only interested in one thing."

"What's that, Tobey?"

"You're too young to know."

She giggled. "You mean kissing?"

"What do you know about kissing?" I asked her.

"I kissed Andy Cowden once at a birthday party."

Fourth graders nowadays were obviously more advanced than I had been at that age. "Did he keep his mouth closed?"

Her eyes grew wide. "Of course!"

"Well, that's the difference." She looked confused, but that was all I intended telling her. She'd be in the fifth grade this year and probably find out those things soon enough.

The change between boys and girls happened so quickly that I'm still confused by it. One day we were friends with the boys, and then it seemed almost overnight we were suddenly adversaries. Charles was the only one who didn't change.

With my class, it happened in the sixth grade. One day boys were passing notes to boys in class and girls were passing notes to girls. Then suddenly boys were passing notes to girls, and on the playground girls were gathering in groups to discuss which boys they liked. All my former buddies started acting differently towards me, and when I showed no personal interest in boys, the girls started treating me like an outcast. Charles and I had always been friends, but it was at that point that we became really close.

Don't get me wrong, I'm not totally abnormal. There have been times I've been interested in a boy. The trouble is, the boys went from being buddies to treating me differently and then back to treating me like a buddy again. I didn't like it when they began to treat me differently, because I didn't know how to respond, and when it started I hadn't matured enough to want to be treated differently. When I finally got around to it, I had missed the boat. None of the boys even took me seriously. I was the oddball, the one who never dated and just hung around with Charles. And most of the time that was just fine with me. But sometimes I thought maybe I was missing something.

Also, I wasn't in the right group. In fact, I wasn't in any group at all, unless Charles and I could be considered a group. Our high school is divided into very specific groups, and if you don't start right out in one, your chances of getting in it later are pretty dim.

There is the Popular Group, which consists of the jocks—those boys who go out for team sports or who at least are friends with the boys who go out for sports—and the girls who look right. In this case, looking right means having long, straight hair and wearing tight sweaters. Not too tight, just a little tight. Too tight and you're in another group entirely—one I won't even bother to explain. This group, the Popular Group, is the one that does most of the dating and has all of the parties.

Then there is the Arty Group. This is mostly the kids who go in for drama and art and music. In this group, the girls wear a lot of black (particularly tights) and a lot of eye makeup. The boys are somewhat strange. This group doesn't date much, but they talk a lot. There are a couple of restaurants in town where they hang out and have deep discussions. You rarely see any of this group at the beach, as they don't seem to go in for tans.

Another group is comprised of the school intellectuals. They are only concerned with making grades and walking away with all the scholastic honors. They run the school newspaper and the literary magazine, and they're very, very serious about everything and seldom smile. If Charles wasn't my best friend, he'd probably be a member of that group.

The rest of the student body, the majority actually, are no group at all. It's just little groups of two or three friends, and they're pretty anonymous. I guess you could say they're like me and Charles, except for one major difference. I'm sure that most of them would jump at the chance to be popular, while Charles and I had chosen to be unpopular. Charles and I considered ourselves individualists.

Riding home from the beach, I planned how I would break the news to my parents. I decided that over dessert would be the best time. Not over dinner, because in that case we might not even get to dessert, and that's my favorite part of the meal. I figured Dad would be pretty proud of me. Mother, seldom being consistent, could react in a number of ways. Neither of them had a clue that I was going to try out for the team. They both knew I practiced kicking the ball a lot, but I think they thought that was just an aberration I would probably soon outgrow.

My plan went awry when Robin opened her mouth the minute we sat down at the table.

"Guess what? Tobey's on the football team."

My parents laughed, and I picked up my fork and began to eat. Maybe Robin would be satisfied with just getting a laugh.

She wasn't. "Listen, I'm serious. I held the ball for her and she kicked it really far and the coach says she can be on the team. You should have seen her, she was so good. Some of the boys were really mad because she was so good. And then we went to the beach, and I swam out to the float five times. Will you take me to the football games so I can see Tobey play? Will you? Huh?"

My first fan.

"You didn't really, did you?" my mother asked me.

"She really did. I saw her," said Robin.

"Tobey, some of those boys are enormous. You're going to get killed," said my mother.

"The kicker doesn't get hurt, Mom."

"You're going to be their kicker?" asked my father.

I nodded.

"You always could kick a football." He should know. He was the one who taught me.

"Have they ever had a girl on the team before?" my mother asked.

"Not that I know of," I said.

A pleased smile spread across her face. "Well, good for you!"

My father didn't look so pleased. "Don't you think playing football is a little unfeminine, Tobey?"

"Dad, you're the one who taught me."

"That's different—you were little then."

"If I were a boy, you wouldn't be acting like this."

"She's right, Frank, you wouldn't," said my mother.

Dad looked a little sheepish, as well he might. If

it hadn't been for him, I probably wouldn't have turned out a tomboy. He finally shrugged. "Well, at least they're not going to mistake you for a boy. You're getting really pretty, sugar, you know that?"

"I am not!" I said, blushing furiously. What did he think, that I never looked in the mirror?

"I think you're pretty, Tobey," said Robin.

"Can't I just finish my dinner in peace?" I asked, getting to work on cutting up my meat. I would have excused myself and left the table at that point, but I knew we were having chocolate cream pie for dessert, and that is my absolute favorite, especially when Mom puts chocolate sprinkles on top.

Right in the middle of dessert, the phone rang and Robin ran off to answer it—it's usually for her or for Mom. The only one I ever talked to was Charles, and since he lives right across the street, we generally talked in person.

Robin came back and said, "It's for you, Tobey —it's a boy."

"Is it Charles?" I asked.

"I *said* it was a *boy.*"

Very funny, I thought as I left the table. I knew very well no boy would be calling me up, but once in a while Charles did call, so it must be him.

I said hello, and then this voice said, "If you don't want your leg broken, you better quit the team."

I very nearly laughed out loud. I knew it was Billy Rafferty disguising his voice, and he didn't scare me one little bit.

"You better watch out, Billy, or I'll kidnap your Kenny doll," I told him, knowing a little bit about threatening phone calls myself.

With that the line was disconnected, and I went back to the table.

"Who was that?" asked Robin.

"Billy Rafferty trying to be funny."

"I saw him at the supermarket the other day," my mother said. "He's getting to be quite a nice-looking boy."

"Billy Rafferty?" I couldn't believe my ears.

"Umm. I remember he was chubby when he was little, but now he's all muscle."

"Even between his ears," I muttered.

When dinner was over, I went to look out the front window to see if Charles was home yet. His mother had taken him down to Chicago to get his braces removed, and he'd said they'd probably be late getting back. Her car was in the driveway, though, so I went across the street to tell him the news.

His mother let me in and I went straight down to the basement, which is where he has his room. He is only the luckiest person I know, because his parents let him fix half the basement of their house up as his own room. It is enormous and cool in the summer and warm in the winter. The other half of the basement has a washer and dryer, so it sometimes gets humid down there, but that's the only drawback.

He has bunk beds down there, and when I used

to be allowed to stay overnight, he let me sleep in the top one. He's got rows and rows of books in shelves, a little laboratory fixed up in a corner with his microscope and all kinds of other stuff, and his weight lifting equipment, which he got for Christmas and which we both use, although sometimes I skip a few days and he never does. He also has his very own color television set. The only thing he doesn't have is his own bathroom, so that the only time he has to go upstairs is to use the bathroom or eat. I would like to have my room in the basement, but my parents said no.

"You are now looking at the new kicker on the varsity team," I told Charles as soon as I walked in his room.

Charles grinned at me, and I had been used to him wearing braces for so long I could hardly believe the change in his appearance.

Now you're probably thinking from the name *Charles* and from what I've said about him that he is some strange-looking boy. That is not the case at all. Charles is very good-looking, with wavy blond hair and eyes the color of faded jeans and a very nicely proportioned body that's gotten even better since he's been working out with weights. He could probably have a lot of girls interested in him if he wanted to. And now, with his braces off and his teeth white and straight and beautiful, I thought he was every bit as good-looking as Wynn Neil, in a different sort of way.

"That's fantastic, Tobey, tell me everything that

happened." This was the moment I had been waiting for all day. I told him every little detail, knowing he was as excited about it as I was. Charles is always very supportive of me, just as I am with him.

"You know, Tobey, this is going to make you the most well-known girl in the school. You'll be notorious!"

"What are you talking about, Charles?"

"This is a first for the school. I'll bet they'll even put your picture in the papers. Very soon everyone in that school is going to know who you are. You know what? You might even become popular!"

I gave him a look of disgust. "No, not popular. I think you were right the first time. I might become notorious, but never popular. The girls have to like you to be popular, and the girls are going to hate me being on the football team." Particularly the cheerleaders, who were some of the most popular girls in the school. It would probably really gall them to have to cheer for a girl.

"All our carefully planned unpopularity going right down the drain."

"Well, don't worry about it, Charles. My notoriety shouldn't affect you."

"I was just kidding. It should be a lot of fun. It'll also give me a good excuse to go to my first football game."

"You better go!"

"Of course I will. I'll be your own private cheering section."

And he would, that's how good a friend he is. Despite the fact that he detests football, I knew he wouldn't miss a game this season.

"What are you going to do about Rafferty? You want me to take care of him for you?"

I looked at him in amazement. "Billy Rafferty has probably got fifty pounds on you, Charles. What were you planning to do, beat him up?"

He grinned. "You know that's not my style. I just thought maybe I could reason with him."

"That would be like trying to reason with a robot."

"Yeah, I guess you're right."

"Anyway, I can handle Billy. The magic words are 'Kenny doll.' All I have to do is say them and he backs off."

"Yeah, I guess that could be pretty embarrassing. I'm glad I never had one, or you probably wouldn't let me hear the end of it."

I gave him a wicked look. "As I recall, Charles, you had a mechanical man."

"That wasn't a doll—that was scientific."

"You used to take it everywhere with you."

"I'm warning you, Tobey—"

"As I recall, you even slept with it."

"Gimme a break, Tobey. I was seven years old!"

I let up on him then, because he was perfectly right. We all sleep with some pretty weird things at seven. I had slept with a mangy-looking stuffed moose at that age. In fact, I was sure I still had him around somewhere.

After that we watched television until it was time for me to go home.

The next day Mom took me and Robin shopping for school clothes at the mall in Glenview. Actually, all three of us were getting school clothes, as Mom teaches at Northwestern University. Since she teaches film, though, she dresses pretty casually—usually in jeans and a black turtleneck sweater.

All three of us dress differently. Mom's the most casual, although I always wear jeans around the house. Robin favors skirts and ruffled blouses, while I go more for the preppy look.

I got a couple of new pairs of cords, one skirt—purchased under duress—several oxford cloth shirt-blouses and two new wool, crew-neck sweaters to wear over them when it got colder. I also got a new pair of leather boots with flat heels. Robin wanted a pair with high heels, but Mom talked her out of them. We also looked at winter coats, but none of us was in the mood to try them on. The stores all seem to get their winter clothes in when it's still hot outside.

Mom also insisted I buy some new bras and panties. When I told her I didn't need any, she said, "You don't want the other football players seeing you in your old underwear, do you?"

I gave her this shocked look and then saw that she was kidding. I started to worry about it, though—like what if I couldn't have my own dressing room? Mom finally settled it for me by suggesting I wear my uniform to and from the games, and that seemed like a good solution.

As usual, Robin wanted a bra, too. This time I stood up for her and said why couldn't she at least have a training bra. Robin was ecstatic when Mom finally agreed. Anyway, I didn't think it was going to be long before Robin really needed one.

I remember Mom trying to get me to wear a bra in the sixth grade and me wanting to hang on to undershirts as long as possible. But I was a tomboy and Robin isn't. Then in the seventh grade, the other girls in gym class made fun of me when I still wore an undershirt, so I finally broke down and got a bra. Now I notice that Mom doesn't even wear a bra anymore, but I still wear them. Not wearing one makes you a little too noticeable to the boys. Mom's pretty small, though, so she looks okay.

Then we went to the dime store and bought school supplies and then we had lunch. Afterwards Mom asked us if we wanted to get our hair cut, and we both said no, so then we went home.

Usually I'm really sorry to see summer end and to have to go back to school, but this year was going to be so exciting, what with playing on the football team, that I could hardly wait for Monday to arrive. I didn't even mind all the shopping the way I usually do, because it meant that in two more days school was going to begin.

On Sunday Charles and I packed a picnic lunch and rode our bikes to the beach for probably the last time that year. Once school starts, no one seems to go to the beach anymore, no matter how warm it is out. We went to my favorite beach, one with a little lighthouse on it, where mostly the Northwestern students hang out. They play a lot of volleyball on the beach, which looks like a lot of fun, but out of deference to Charles, I try not even to watch.

Charles dumped his towel down in one of the less crowded areas and took off to look for specimens. I left his towel where he dumped it and spread out my own out carefully to get as little sand as possible on top of it. I took off my sneakers and shorts and then pulled my shirt over my head. I wanted to get in some running and swimming, but first I felt like just relaxing on the sand and thinking about being on the football team. So far I hadn't had much time all to myself to think about it.

I was right in the middle of one of my favorite fantasies, the one where the team is losing by two points and there's only ten seconds left in the game and the coach calls in the field goal team. I put on my helmet and trot out on the field and all the kids in the stands start to go wild, yelling, "Kick that ball! Kick that ball!" I dig my toe in the grass while the ball is placed, and then I start to run. My toe really connects with the ball, and everyone in the stands holds his breath as the ball goes sailing right over the goal post for three points and we win the game. The crowd goes crazy cheering and stamping, and the other players surround me, patting me on the back, then finally lifting me up and carrying me in triumph off the field. Right there is where the fantasy usually stops, because I don't think they'd carry me into the locker room, and I don't even know what the locker room looks like.

Anyway, I was going over that fantasy in my mind, only this time for some reason it ended with Wynn Neil putting me on his shoulders and then carrying me around the field. This was kind of a surprise to me, as I couldn't remember ever being specific about any of the players before. Usually they were just a blur. But when I thought about it, I knew I'd like to be riding around on Wynn's shoulders.

The funny part of it is that the first time he had ever spoken to me had been when I tried out for the team. I don't think he even knew I was alive before then. He had always been this older, popular boy who was untouchable, as far as I was concerned. Only now I'd be getting to know him.

I stopped myself for a minute. It was a total impossibility to think Wynn Neil would ever like me; I was deluding myself to even fantasize about it. First of all, he just happened to be going steady with the prettiest girl in the school, Suzanna Meredith. And not only was she so pretty that I stared at her whenever I saw her, but she was also very nice and friendly . . . for a senior. And they made the most perfect-looking couple I've ever seen. So for me to think for even a moment that me and Wynn Neil could ever be more than just teammates was just stupid, unproductive thinking.

Nevertheless, I started thinking about it again

anyway. I think I had been secretly getting a crush on him ever since the tryouts.

It was right then as I was thinking about Wynn Neil that these four college guys spread out a couple of blankets not two feet from mine and took a sixpack of beer out of a backpack. Beer is not allowed at the beach, but I guess they weren't worried about getting caught.

One of the guys, a blond with a bushy mustache, noticed me and held out a can of beer in my direction. "You want one?" he asked me.

"No thanks," I said, flattered that he'd offer me a beer. I thought of adding that I couldn't because I was in training, but then figured that would be bragging, so I didn't say it.

He was smiling at me. Well, to be perfectly honest, he was mostly smiling in the direction of my bikini, and that made me a little nervous, so I rolled over on my stomach and turned my head away.

"Hey, don't be mad," he yelled over at me. I could hear his friends laughing. "What year are you, anyway?" he asked when I didn't say anything.

I turned my head back. "I'm a sophomore."

"Yeah? Me too!"

Fine, I thought, only he was in college and I was only in high school—which he should have been able to see if he was perceptive at all. Nevertheless, I didn't jump right in and tell him that I was still in high school.

"What are you majoring in?" he asked next, and right then I knew the game was up, because I didn't even know what he was talking about. Instead of replying, I just gave a shrug, which is kind of hard to manage when you're lying on your stomach.

"What are you doing tonight? You want to come to a party?"

I couldn't very well tell him that my parents would never allow me to go to a college party; I hadn't even been to a high school one yet. I realized I was getting in a little over my head. He was flirting with me, and I've never really learned how to flirt.

"Sorry, I can't," I told him, and then was relieved to see that Charles was back and sitting down next to me.

"Who are they?" he asked me.

"How would I know?"

I could see the college guys get up and run into the water.

"You were talking to them, weren't you?"

"They were talking to me, Charles. I didn't start it."

"What did they want?"

"I was invited to a party tonight."

"They invited *you?*" My sentiments exactly, but not what I wanted to hear from Charles.

"Are you surprised some boy would ask me out?"

"They're kind of old, aren't they?"

"What's the difference? I turned him down."

Charles was scowling, and it wasn't because he was staring into the sun.

"I've been thinking maybe I'd start dating this year," I said to Charles, wondering what his reaction would be.

"Who's going to ask you out?"

He was perfectly right. Nobody had asked me out yet, but somehow his attitude was really annoying me. "Well, I *will* be getting to know the football team pretty well."

Charles muttered something I couldn't hear. When I asked him to repeat it, he said, "If you really want to go out, Tobey, I'll take you out."

"That's not going out, Charles; we already go everywhere together. I'm talking about a date."

"All right. I'll ask you for a date. Do you want to go out next weekend?"

"Charles, you're my very best friend, and you don't date a friend. Anyway, there's no way I could feel the slightest bit romantic about you. I know you too well."

"Maybe I should start dating, too." I know he was trying to make me jealous, but it just wouldn't work.

"That would probably be a good idea."

"But you're the only girl I like."

"That's because I'm the only girl you know!"

"Yeah, maybe you're right. I think I'll wait 'til next year, though, when I can drive a car."

"Charles, if I do start dating, and I'm not really positive about that yet, you'll still be my best friend. There's no other boy I'd really want to talk to."

I could tell that Charles had already lost interest in the conversation, so I put on my sneakers and began to run down the beach. It had only been a thought anyway. Probably no one ever would ask me out.

3

In some ways, the first week back at school was the most traumatic of my life.

Our high school is pretty large. There are ten home rooms with 250 students in each, so you can see there are a whole lot of kids in the school I don't even know. I know all the kids who went to Willard Elementary School, and most of the kids who were at Haven School when I was in the seventh and eighth grades there. But half the high school is comprised of students from South Evanston, and unless they are well-known for something, I don't even know who they are.

I was taking English and geometry and Spanish and world history and biology and girls' chorus, which is a snap—you get two credits for just showing up and opening your mouth, whether you can sing or not, and I most definitely can't. I figured the only subject I would like even marginally was geometry. It was the only class Charles and I would have together. We didn't even get lunch period together, which meant I'd probably have to eat alone all year. In the cafeteria you sit with the group you belong to, and my group consisted of me and Charles.

The first day back at school a very strange thing happened to me in the cafeteria. I had gone through the line and had my lettuce sandwich and Jell-O and chocolate milk on my tray and was walking down the aisle to find an empty spot at one of the tables when I passed by where a bunch of the football players were sitting. I wasn't even looking in their direction, just straight ahead and minding my own business, but one of the guys called out, "Hey, Tobey, how're you doing?" Then a couple of the others said, "Hey, Tobey," and I looked over at them and said, "How're you doing, guys?" and I wouldn't have thought any more about it except when I passed the table where the popular girls in my class sat, they all turned to look at me. I could see they were confused over why I was getting so much attention from the jocks.

Katie Lou Slight, who is the most popular sophomore girl—mainly because she's the meanest and bossiest and knows how to manipulate the other girls, and also, to be honest, she's very, very pretty—slowed down by my table when she was leaving the cafeteria and said, "Hi, Tobey, did you have a good summer?"

Now I realize this doesn't sound startling, but you'd just have to know Katie Lou to understand how surprised I was. First of all, in our entire freshman year, she never even spoke one word to me. And before that, during junior high, which is when I first met her, all she ever did was criticize me. She was almost directly responsible for my deciding to wear a bra. She started calling me a baby for still wearing an undershirt, and pretty soon the other girls in gym were calling me that until I finally broke down and began wearing one. And then I think she regretted it, because it turned out I had more to put in a bra than she did. In fact, now you could consider her almost flat-chested, because she hasn't grown at all since the seventh grade. Not that this means anything to me, but it seems to be very important to the popular girls.

Anyway, I was so unnerved at being spoken to by her that I couldn't think of anything to say. When her friends behind her also said hi or smiled at me as they passed by, I just sat there eating my Jell-O and wondering, why me?

The fastest way for a girl to become popular in our school is for a popular boy to like her. So, since most of the football players are automatically popular just because they play football (I say *most,* not *all,* because I couldn't conceivably think of obnoxious Billy Rafferty as being popular), I could only assume Katie Lou had surmised that the boys liked me, so she wasn't going to take any chances by ignoring me. That kind of made me laugh when I thought about it. I wouldn't have minded a popular boy liking me—Wynn Neil came to mind immediately—but I really could have lived without attention from Katie Lou and her cohorts. I wouldn't join their group if they begged me!

After lunch I had geometry. Charles had saved me a seat in the back of the room. Mostly the good students sit in the front rows and they're always raising their hands, while the poor, inattentive ones sit in the very last row, where they can goof off and maybe even sleep. But even though Charles is a good student, he's not the kind who likes to ask or answer a lot of questions. He's willing to sit at the back with me, so we can pass notes and generally make observations on the class. I'm kind of an in-between student. I do my homework and do pretty well on tests, but I seldom pay any attention in class because mostly it's very boring. Also I hate having to sit still for such long stretches.

When I grow up, I'd hate to have one of those jobs where you have to sit in an office all day, which is why I'm tentatively planning on becoming an explorer of some kind. If this doesn't work out, my next choice would be a gym teacher. Charles wants to do research of some kind, but then he can sit for very long periods of time without fidgeting.

I wrote a note to Charles telling him about Katie Lou acting so friendly to me in the cafeteria. He kind of chuckled when he read it, then wrote me back saying, "Next thing you know, you'll be found giggling with a group of girls." I wrote back NEVER in very large letters, and after that I let Charles take notes on what the teacher was saying while I sat and daydreamed about football practice that day.

It turned out even more exciting than my daydreams. The very best part was getting my very own uniform, complete with shoulder pads and helmet and everything. The rest of the team was already out on the field practicing while I was being fitted, but the coach came in to talk to me. I told him about how I'd decided to wear my uniform to and from the games so that I wouldn't need to be in the locker room, and he thought that was a very good idea. He told me I might get some flak from the boys about my being on the team but not to pay any attention to them, because he was sure they'd stop being resentful as soon as I started scoring some points for the team.

I wasn't worried about the team. I wasn't even worried about Billy Rafferty. He could be as disagreeable as he wanted. I wasn't going to let it bother me at all. In fact, if he didn't watch out, I was going to start calling him Kenny, after his doll. That should shut him up in a hurry.

I can't begin to describe how I felt when I ran out on the field for the first time in my uniform. I had always wanted a football uniform. Every Christmas I asked for one, and although my mother never minded buying me footballs and even a helmet, I had never received a complete uniform before.

What I hadn't counted on was all the girls who turned out to watch the boys practice. There were clusters of them sitting in the bleachers, and one cluster, I couldn't help noticing, was Katie Lou

Slight and her friends. At first I think they thought I was just another of the boys, albeit smaller than the others. But when the coach called me over, I was pretty close to where Katie Lou was sitting, and out of the corner of my eye I could see that she recognized me. Well, I hadn't expected to be able to keep it a secret for very long.

"Ted's going to hold the ball for you while you practice place kicks," the coach said to me. When I told him I didn't know who Ted was, he pointed him out to me.

I guess Coach McKeever picked Ted for the job because he was one of the boys who didn't seem to resent my presence. He was a senior and turned out to be very nice and helpful. I spent maybe forty minutes with him kicking one ball after another. Wynn Neil was practicing throwing the ball to his receivers. Then we practiced punt returns, with me doing the punting, and some of the guys said things like "Good kick, Tobey," to me, while others, like Billy Rafferty, acted as though I were invisible. Which was just fine with me. I'll bet what annoyed him more than anything was the fact that the kicker doesn't get tackled. I'll just bet Billy would have loved to tackle me and maybe break both my legs.

Off to the side of the field, the cheerleaders were practicing. I had forgotten all about them. They were all juniors and seniors, and the head cheerleader, Karen Woodrow, was one of the most popular girls in the school, second only to Wynn's girlfriend, Suzanna. But while I think Suzanna is all right, Karen is something else. She's a blonde, naturally, with a little help from Sun-Up, and to give some indication of how sharp she is, her major ambition in life is to grow up to be a Dallas Cowgirl. For reasons that never cease to amaze me, the boys all think she's wonderful. But then if the school ever held a sweater contest, Karen would win by several inches.

At the conclusion of practice, we had to run a few laps around the field, which made me glad I had been doing a lot of running at the beach during the summer. At first I thought it was like a race, and I quickly passed most of the team until I got to Billy, and he yelled, "Look at the show-off, will you?" and I heard some of the guys laugh. Then I realized that no one was trying to beat anyone and I slowed down, but not near Billy. After that, the coach took us all into the gym, where he went over team strategy. I wasn't sure whether I was supposed to be there or not, as the kicker doesn't really have to run any plays, but no one told me to leave, so I sat at the back and just listened.

Our opening game, scheduled for next Saturday, was against Oak Park, one of the toughest teams in the Suburban League. One of the reasons they're so tough is that about 90 percent of their team is black. Another reason is that they play rough and dirty. When we play Oak Park, there are always a lot of injuries, unlike New Trier, where it's almost like playing a girls' team. Not that I think girls can't play football, but they're just not as large as the boys for the most part.

This would be an away game, which would mean I'd have to take the bus there with the team. I was sorry about having to do that so soon, as I was sure I'd be sitting all by myself and totally ignored by the boys. Plus they'd probably feel constrained to watch their language in front of me, even though I know all the same words they know. The difference is I don't use them in everyday conversation. I just think them to myself sometimes when I get mad.

When we were all finished for the day, I went to the girls' washroom to change back into my school clothes. I was given a nylon athletic bag with EVANSTON stenciled on the side and I put my uniform in that. Instead of putting it in my school locker, I decided to take it home. I couldn't wait for my family and Charles to see me in it.

I had missed all the school buses and would have to walk a few blocks to downtown Evanston in order to get a bus home.

As I was cutting across the parking lot, I unfortunately passed by Billy Rafferty and some of his friends getting into a car.

"Hey, Tobey," he yelled at me, "you getting your thrills from playing with the big boys?"

"You getting yours from making anonymous phone calls?" I yelled right back. I probably should have just ignored him, but that's not my style.

His friends all looked at him when I said that, and I could see he was trying to make up his mind what to do. Then he started walking towards me with this really menacing manner, his friends right with him. I put down my bag and stood there with my hands on my hips, daring him on. I didn't really think he had the nerve to do anything to me.

He was about six feet from me when this red Toyota pulled up on the other side of me. Wynn Neil looked out the window. "Can I give you a ride home, Tobey?" he asked, taking in the situation.

"I can handle Billy Rafferty," I told him, which was sheer foolishness on my part. Billy must have a hundred pounds on me.

"I'm sure you can, Tobey. All I wanted to know was did you want a ride home. You live north, don't you?"

I nodded. "I live on Lawndale."

"That's near me. Why don't you get in?"

I looked over then and saw that he already had two boys in the back seat and one in the front. It would be a loss of dignity for one player to be seen sitting on another player's lap, which was where I would end up, I was sure.

Billy meanwhile was standing there glaring at me, although what he had in mind I'm sure I don't know. Even a bully like Billy wouldn't be likely to take on a small girl, especially with the other guys looking on.

"Did you want something, Billy?" I asked him sweetly.

His face was almost as red as his hair, which is the way it used to get when he was a kid and I beat him at something. "It'll wait," he muttered, thinking no doubt he was scaring me, which he wasn't.

I gave an indifferent shrug, then picked up my

bag. "Thanks, Wynn, but I don't think you have room for me," I said.

Mitchell Waters, who was sitting in the front seat, opened the door and got out, saying that he could sit in the back with the other guys.

Well, not wanting to make even a bigger production of the whole thing, I went and got in the car beside Wynn. The back seat looked very crowded. Toyotas aren't that big, and two of the guys were tackles and one was a linebacker. I think the rear end of the car must have been sinking to the ground.

Wynn pulled out of the parking lot. "Why's Rafferty got it in for you?" he asked me.

"I think Billy's got it in for everybody," I told him, getting a few chuckles from the back seat.

"He's not a bad guy," said Wynn. "Did you two go out together or something?"

Me go out with Billy Rafferty? What a laugh! If Billy Rafferty and I were stranded together on some desert island, I think we'd end up killing each other.

"We used to fight a lot when we were kids," I told him.

"Well, I wish you two could quit fighting now. The team plays a lot better when everybody's friends."

I was sorry to hear that, as I knew it wasn't possible for me and Billy ever to be friends. "He's probably not the only one who doesn't want me on the team," I remarked, hoping of course that they'd all say, "Oh, no, we all want you!"

One of the boys in the back seat said, "We don't mind you, Tobey; it was just kind of a surprise, you know?"

Yeah, I knew.

"Anyway, it's not like you're out there playing with us," said Mitchell. "All you're doing is kicking."

I would have liked to argue about that, to tell them how important the kicker was, but I thought it more tactful at that point to let it go. Anyway, I was getting a free ride home, which meant I should at least be polite.

Wynn asked me if I minded if they stopped for a Coke. Of course I said no, so when we got to Central Street, he pulled into a drive-in where most of the high school crowd hangs out. I ordered a Coke, and the rest of them ordered hamburgers and fries, too. I wouldn't have minded a hamburger, but I knew I'd be eating dinner soon, and I didn't want my mother to think my lack of appetite was due to football practice and put up a fuss.

There were all kinds of kids from school there, and naturally they all saw me sitting in the front seat with Wynn, which couldn't hurt my reputation at all. Boys kept dropping by the car and talking in the window, and the girls were all checking us out. I just sat there acting cool, as though I always drove around with Wynn. I was really sorry when they were finished and we left. Soon enough, though, the whole school would find out what I was doing driving around with part of the team.

It turned out Wynn only lived a few blocks from

me, and so he dropped me off last. Once I was in the car all alone with him, I got really shy and tongue-tied. He had the radio on, though, so I figured maybe he wouldn't notice.

When he pulled up in front of my house, I thanked him for the ride and started to get out.

"Be glad to give you a ride home after practice every day," he told me.

"You don't have to do that," I told him.

"What's the difference? You're right on the way."

"Thanks, I'll give you money for gas."

He laughed. "That's more than the others do."

I got out my wallet, but he waved it aside. "Forget it, Tobey. I have to drive this far anyway. Listen, I'm having a party a week from Saturday, if you want to come. The whole team will be there. We have a home game that day, so I thought it would be a good time."

"Sure, thanks," I told him, getting out of the car in a daze. A party at Wynn Neil's house? I couldn't believe this was really happening. My first high school party, and it was being given by a senior and the most popular boy in the school. I'd probably be the only sophomore to even go to it.

And then I wondered if maybe he was asking me like a date or something. But I really didn't think I was getting that lucky. He had to be asking me because the whole team was going and he was too nice to leave me out. I was sure Suzanna would be there with him, along with most of the popular girls in the school. And then I remembered that Billy

Rafferty would also be there, and the thrill subsided a little.

As soon as I got in the house, Robin told me dinner was almost ready, but I told her I wanted to change my clothes first and would be right down.

She followed me up to my room. I figured that since she had a hand in my making the team, she should be allowed to see me in my uniform first. I got out of my school clothes and even remembered to hang them up, then took my football uniform out of the bag and put it on.

"Gee, Tobey, you look just like a boy in it," she told me.

This time when I put on my helmet, I shoved all my hair up under it. She was right. I did look like a boy, if you didn't look close. It was such a bulky uniform that it obscured my figure completely.

The only thing wrong with our uniforms is that they're the same colors as our school colors, which are bright blue and orange and one of the worst color combinations I can imagine. I wish we had purple and white like Northwestern or green and gold like Notre Dame, but we're stuck with blue and orange and that's that. At least my number was absolutely perfect: I'm number 4, and that's one of my favorite numbers. I like all the even numbers and none of the odd. If I had gotten 3, I would have felt jinxed. But 4 was, I thought, a good sign.

My parents were really surprised to see me come to dinner in my uniform. My dad made me turn around and then said I looked very professional except for my shoes. I was wearing my running shoes.

I told him they didn't have football shoes to fit me and that I preferred wearing my own shoes anyway, because they were the ones I was used to kicking in.

My mother just said, "Very nice," and then asked me to remove my helmet while I ate. We were having meatloaf, and I was sorry I hadn't had a hamburger after all. Even though they're made out of the exact same kind of meat, I just love hamburgers, and I don't like meatloaf much at all.

They asked us both about our first days back at school. After Robin got through talking, I told them all about football practice.

"How about your classes?" Mom asked me.

"I don't know—it's too soon to tell. But listen, I've been invited to a party at Wynn Neil's a week from Saturday night."

"Do we know him?" asked my father.

"It's not a date. He's the quarterback, and the whole team's invited. Plus a lot of other people, too, I suppose."

My mother seemed pleased. "Well, your first party . . . we'll have to get you something nice to wear."

"I think probably everyone will just be in jeans," I told her. What she had in mind, I'm sure, was a dress.

"I imagine so," said my mother. "That's all they wear at Northwestern, anyway."

It was still light out after dinner, so I talked Robin into going outside with me and holding the ball while I kicked a few in the street. I didn't really need the practice, but I wanted all the neighbors to see me in my uniform. A lot of the little boys who live on our block came out, and I threw the ball to a few of them. Then Charles came out, and I took a break and sat on his front porch with him. They have a really neat front porch with a glider I like to sit in. Our house doesn't have a front porch, just a back screened-in porch. And we don't have a glider.

"How'd it go at practice?" he asked me.

I told him every detail and, to show what a good friend he is, he paid attention to every word, even though I know he must have been bored. Then I told him about the party.

"Are you going?"

"Sure I'm going. The whole team's going."

Just then I saw a familiar-looking, beat-up green car pass by with a familiar-looking redhead at the wheel. It was driving slowly as it passed my house. I poked Charles in the ribs.

"Look, that's Billy Rafferty. What's he doing driving by my house?"

"I think you're getting paranoid, Tobey."

"Just because I think he's out to get me doesn't mean I'm paranoid," I told him.

"That's exactly what it means."

"No, it's only paranoid if it's not true. Even Wynn noticed Billy has it in for me."

58

"You and Wynn are getting pretty friendly, aren't you?"

"He's being very nice to me."

"I wonder why."

"Probably because he's a very nice boy."

Charles looked doubtful.

"Charles, you can't honestly believe Wynn Neil would be interested in *me*."

"No, I guess not."

Sometimes Charles says the exact opposite of what I want to hear.

Right about then we saw the green car coming from the opposite direction, and when it slowed down in front of my house, I yelled out, "Get off my street, Rafferty!"

"He lives on this street, too," Charles pointed out.

Maybe so, but Billy had no business driving by my house. The car stopped and Billy's head looked in our direction. "Making out with your boyfriend, Tobey?"

Disgusting boys like Billy only have one thing on their little minds. "If I am, that makes you a Peeping Tom," I yelled back, noticing too late the look of dismay on Charles's face. I could see I was embarrassing him and I was sorry about that. But it was all Billy's fault for starting it.

I could hear Billy's annoyingly raucous laugh. In fact, the whole neighborhood probably heard it.

"He's probably your speed," Billy jeered at me, and that was the absolute limit.

"What did you say?" I practically screamed at him.

"You heard me!"

In a flash I was out of the glider and down the stairs of the porch. Halfway to his car I was yelling at him, "Get out of your car and say that, Rafferty!" I was so furious I could barely control myself. They say redheads have tempers, but I'd match mine to Billy Rafferty's any day.

Of course I hadn't expected him to actually get out of his car. I guess I had been hoping he'd take off fast, making a big point of burning rubber on the way. Instead, the car door opened and Billy got out, then stood casually leaning back against the side of the car. He was wearing old faded jeans and a torn t-shirt and looked menacing standing there. Menacing and very, very large.

"He's probably your speed," he said in a low voice, taking me up on my dare.

With the firm conviction that I had to protect Charles's good name, I charged towards Billy. I don't really know whether I planned to punch him in the face or what, but my hands were in fists and I had them out in front of me. The fact that Billy was now laughing infuriated me even more.

As soon as I got close enough to hit him, he grabbed both my wrists and pinned them with one large hand, leaving me so frustrated I could have screamed. I started to kick him, but he just laughed harder at my attempts.

I don't know whether it was fortunate or unfortunate, but at that moment my mother came out of the front door of our house and yelled across the street to me, "Is anything the matter over there, Tobey?"

It only took about a second for Billy to release my wrists, straighten up, and look over the top of the car at my mother. "Hello there, Mrs. Tyler," he said to her, just as nice and polite as you please.

"Oh, hello, Billy. I hear you and Tobey are going to be teammates."

"That's right, Mrs. Tyler," said Billy, with this great big smile on his devious face.

"You better come in soon and do your homework," said my mother before going in the house.

"You are the most despicable person I have ever known in my whole entire life," I said to Billy with the very nastiest scowl I could manage.

"You know something, Tobey? You look ridiculous in that uniform," he said, then he got back in his car and drove off before I could think of a cutting retort. I had forgotten all about having my uniform on and did feel kind of stupid having him see me wear it when I wasn't supposed to.

"You really don't know how to handle him," came Charles's voice from the porch.

"Oh, yeah? I didn't see you doing anything."

"What did you want me to do, rush out and punch him in the nose? First of all, I'm a pacifist, and second of all, he's three times my size. But that doesn't mean I need you to protect me. The best way to handle someone of his mentality is to just ignore him. Show-offs like Rafferty just can't stand being ignored."

That made it sound like me and Billy Rafferty are alike, because I also can't stand being ignored. And what's more, Charles knows it. He has also, on more than one occasion, accused me of being a show-off.

"You know something, Charles?" I said. "Billy was wrong. You're not my speed. I at least stand up for myself!" I was really ticked off at Charles and didn't even bother to say goodnight. I crossed the street slowly, waiting for him to call out and say something to me, but by the time I had got to my house he was still silent, so I went inside and slammed the door. Very hard so that he would be sure to hear it.

It was no big deal. Charles and I fought a lot, but neither of us carried grudges, and the argument would be forgotten in the morning.

I went to the kitchen to get an apple and ran into my mother.

"Did Billy Rafferty come over to see you?" she asked me.

"I guess you could say that."

"Well," she said in this all-knowing way.

"Well nothing! I can't stand him and he knows it."

"He seems to be turning into a fine young man," she said as she left the kitchen.

Which just goes to show how perceptive mothers are when it comes to boys!

4

On Tuesday Billy Rafferty just happened to be in the cafeteria during my lunch hour, which I don't think is his. That means the only reason he was there was to annoy me. Charles would say that was another indication of my paranoia, but he would be wrong, as this is what happened.

I was walking down the aisle with my tray and Billy Rafferty, quite deliberately, put his foot out and tripped me. On purpose. I went sprawling on the floor, my tray making quite a clatter, and of course a good part of the school saw this happen. My Jell-O got spilled, but my sandwich was okay and my milk carton was still intact. I got to my feet and made sure I was all right. My biggest worry was that he might have injured my kicking foot, but it seemed to be okay. I picked up my tray and set it on the table where Billy was sitting, leaving the Jell-O where it was on the floor.

There was kind of a hushed silence in the cafeteria, and I could see Billy and his friends waiting to see what I'd do. I was so mad I was almost in tears. Only almost, though, because I have trained myself never to cry. I really cannot abide crybabies.

I very slowly, very calmly, opened my carton of chocolate milk, then before he could stop me, I poured it all over Billy Rafferty's head. I didn't even stop to think what a foolish move this was on my part. I mean, I probably could've been thrown out of school for doing something like this, and that would mean I'd be off the team.

As his friends sat there open-mouthed and Billy sat there dripping chocolate milk, one of the cafeteria monitors came charging down the aisle. "What's happening here? Who did this?" he asked when he got to us. I waited for Billy to jump at the chance to get me in trouble. I'm sure the whole point of his tripping me was to make me reciprocate in a way that would be sure to get me in trouble.

I was really surprised when Billy merely shrugged and said, "Nothing. It was an accident, that's all. I'll clean it up."

Before any further questions could be asked, I picked up my tray and started back down the aisle. As I passed the table where Katie Lou and her friends were sitting, I heard Katie Lou say in a loud voice, "Well, what do you expect of a jock," and I knew she was referring to me, not Billy. Now that she knew the reason the boys were talking to me was because I was on the football team and not because they personally liked me, she was back to making fun of me. Which was okay with me; I don't trust Katie Lou when she's being friendly.

I was looking around for an empty table when I saw Karen Woodrow motioning to me to come sit with her. She was sitting with the other senior cheerleaders and a few of the other senior girls. I thought, what the heck, probably nobody else wanted to sit with me, so I took the empty chair across from her and sat down. Even though I considered her a very dumb blonde, at least she wasn't mean like Katie Lou.

"Do you and Billy Rafferty have a feud going?" she asked me.

"I guess you could say that."

"He doesn't like me much, either," she said, giving me a smile of commiseration. "Of course, that's because I wouldn't go out with him."

"I can understand why," I told her.

"Oh, it's just because he's a year behind me. If it weren't for that, I probably would have. I think he's kind of sexy."

Which just reinforced my view of her as a dumb blonde.

I didn't think she invited me to sit with them for my scintillating conversation, so I started to eat my lettuce sandwich. I was too embarrassed to go back through the line and get more Jell-O and milk.

"You know, Tobey, we're quite excited about having a girl on the football team." This was another of the cheerleaders speaking, but Karen was nodding in agreement.

"You are?" I asked, pretty surprised to hear that.

"What we're going to do," said Karen, "is compose a cheer just for you. So far, though, we're having a lot of trouble finding anything to rhyme with 'Tobey.'"

I thought about that while I finished my sandwich, but I couldn't come up with anything that rhymed with my name, either—except maybe Moby, like the book *Moby Dick*, but I didn't think the name of a whale would be appropriate for a football cheer.

Katie Lou and her friends passed by then, and Katie Lou looked absolutely furious that I was sitting with the popular senior girls. I pretended I didn't even see her.

"Well anyway, Tobey, we wanted you to know we're behind you, and if Billy Rafferty continues to give you trouble, just let us know and we'll put the freeze on him."

Next period I told Charles all about what had happened. He said my life was getting so complicated it was beginning to sound like a soap opera. He also said that pouring chocolate milk over Billy's head was putting myself on his level and that I should try to act more adult and just ignore him.

The only trouble with that advice is that I have a lot of trouble ignoring people. And it had given me a great deal of satisfaction to soak Billy in chocolate.

Nothing much else happened until Friday. The football practices went well, Wynn drove me home every day and I continued to sit with the cheerleaders in the cafeteria. It was just slightly better than eating alone. One of the school intellectuals, Coleman Brown, asked if he could interview me for the school paper. I told him I'd have to ask permission of Coach McKeever first. He said he'd get back to me.

On Friday we were excused from our last period class to attend a pep rally in the auditorium. What I didn't know until the period before that, when I received a memo in class from the coach, was that I had to sit on the stage with the rest of the team during the rally.

I was so scared my knees were shaking when I walked up the steps to the stage to take my seat. I was hoping at least to be able to sit in the back row, but all those seats were taken and I was stuck sitting in the front. The auditorium filled up with hundreds and hundreds of faces, all, I was sure, looking right in my direction. I kept my eyes down on my feet and tried to pretend I was somewhere else. *Anywhere* else.

First the principal made an announcement, then turned the pep rally over to Coach McKeever. He told the school what a good team we had this year and that he was hoping to see all of them at Oak Park the next day for the first game of the season. Then he called out our names one by one. Each player had to stand up while the audience cheered. When he got to my name, he said that they were very pleased, for the first time in history, to have a girl on the team. When he said that I could hear someone behind me make an obscene noise, and I knew it was Billy Rafferty. Then I had to stand up. There was a lot of cheering and also some whistling, which really embarrassed me, and I know I turned red.

After that we sang the school fight song and then Karen got up—the cheerleaders were also on the stage but on the other side—and said she was going to teach the school some new cheers. She and the other cheerleaders demonstrated a couple of new cheers, and then they did one just for me. It went like this:

> Tobey, Tobey, does it all!
> Every time she kicks the ball!
> Tobey! Tobey! Tobey!

Pretty soon she had the whole school doing it—everyone but me, that is. I just didn't think I should be yelling out my own name. It would be just like voting for myself in an election.

I thought the assembly would never end, but it finally did and I went to my locker to get my football uniform and change for practice.

When I got out on the field, Billy Rafferty and a bunch of his friends were waiting for me. With hands on hips, they began kicking their legs and acting just like cheerleaders. It would have been pretty funny, but then they began to chant:

Tobey, Tobey, does it all!
In the classroom, in the hall,
Even in the shower stall!
Naughty, naughty, Tobey!

I felt like putting my strong foot to good purpose by kicking Billy where it would hurt the most. Why is it that boys turn out so dirty-minded when they come from the same kind of homes as girls? I happened to know that Billy had two very nice older sisters. I just wished they'd beaten some sense into him when he had been younger.

"Very good, Billy," I said to him sarcastically. "You actually found three words that rhyme. Keep it up and you might even graduate from high school."

I could see by his face that he was disappointed I hadn't rushed him with my fists again or maybe even burst into tears. I just calmly walked away from him and over to Ted, who was waiting to hold the ball for me.

"Way to go, kid," said Ted, which made me feel a whole lot better. Except for Billy and a few of his friends, all the other guys on the team were being very supportive.

At the end of practice the coach gave us a pep talk about team spirit and everyone pulling together, and I looked over at Billy and saw he was looking at me. Then the coach saw we were looking at each other and said, "Yes, even you two," and everyone laughed. One thing was true, though: I liked being on the team even more than I disliked Billy. I would be glad to try to get along if he would also. Fat chance of that, though!

That night I could hardly sleep; I was so excited about playing in my first game the next day. It was just like Christmas Eve when I was a kid and too excited about what Santa Claus was going to bring, so that sleep seemed never to come. When it finally did come, I had the first nightmare I had had in years, since I was really little and used to dream about foxes being under my bed.

And who was in my nightmare? You guessed it—Billy Rafferty. In my dream I was late to school the next day, and the team bus left without me. I was standing there feeling as though it were the end of the world, knowing that because I missed the game I'd be thrown off the team and my dream of being a football player would be shattered forever. And as I was standing there, Billy Rafferty pulled up in his green car and rolled down the window.

"How come you're not on the bus?" he asked me, a sly smile on his face.

I told him about missing the bus and asked him if he'd give me a ride, but he just laughed and rolled up the window and took off real fast.

Then I woke up. At first I thought the dream was real and that I had missed the game, but then I realized it was still Friday night. It was only a dream. I silently cursed Billy Rafferty for not only trying to make my waking life miserable, but now also for invading my dreams and turning them into nightmares.

In actuality I was at the school a full half hour before any of the other players, and I was already tired of standing around by the time the team bus arrived. The cheerleaders also were there, and when we started to get on the bus, I wondered if I should ride with the girls, who had been pretty friendly with me, or ride with the team of which I was a part. I solved the problem by riding up front alone, across the aisle from the coaches. I figured up there Billy Rafferty wouldn't dare bother me. The cheerleaders were clear at the back of the bus practicing their cheers, and the players were all joking back and forth trying not to be nervous about the game. I just looked out the window, watching the scenery going by.

The coach asked me about five times, "You're not nervous are you, Tobey?" And I wasn't at first, but after he asked five times I began to be. What would happen if I missed any of the kicks? Would they throw me off the team? I didn't really think so, since the kicker last year always missed and they still used him. But he wasn't a girl; maybe they'd use my missing as an excuse to get rid of me, since they hadn't wanted a girl in the first place.

When we got to Oak Park, there was a big turnout for the game. Their side of the stands was filled to capacity, but our side was pretty full-up, too. Lots of the kids had come out to see our first game. I knew my parents and Robin and Charles were up there somewhere, but I didn't turn around to find them.

I stood on the sidelines with the coaches while

the rest of the players went out on the field to practice. Oak Park's coach came over and said, "I hear you have a girl on the team, Mac, but I don't believe it." Then he saw me. "At least I didn't believe it until now."

Coach McKeever grinned. "She's my secret weapon, John."

"What do you do, put her in the game and hope my boys are too gentlemanly to tackle her?"

Coach McKeever gave a bark of laughter. "I'm not an idiot—your players are never gentlemen."

Then it was time for the national anthem, and I stood with the team as it was sung. After that came the opening kick, and that opening kick was going to be kicked by me. I was going to be seen by everyone on the very first play of the game.

I put on my helmet and ran out on the field, then got into position to make the kickoff. I could hear some cheers from our side of the field; from Oak Park's side I heard some whistles, which didn't please me very much. Then I stopped hearing everything as I concentrated on kicking the ball.

Ted was holding the ball and I got off a good kick, so good that their receiver only got out to the 18-yard line with it. Again I heard some cheers for me as I ran off the field. It was a very heady experience hearing those cheers. I couldn't remember ever being cheered for anything before. I couldn't wait to get out there again and actually score a point.

Our defense was out on the field, and I stood

near Wynn on the sidelines. "Nice kick, Tobey," he said. "I don't think they'll score from way back there." None of the other guys said anything to me, but I guess they were too intent on the game.

Coach McKeever was pacing back and forth, chewing gum furiously, even though not much was happening on the field. I think he watches the coaches on the pro games and models himself after them.

Oak Park did score, though, and took a long time doing it, so ten minutes into the game we were behind by 7 points. Then they got to kick, and I was pleased to see their kicker didn't kick it nearly as far as I had.

Wynn and the offense took the field, and I couldn't wait for them to either score a touchdown so I could kick the extra point, or either get it far enough down the field so I could kick a field goal. Neither happened, and even though I got to go out and punt the ball, that was no consolation. I wanted our team to score!

Oak Park had the ball again, and their quarterback, who has the best arm in the league, quickly got his team out to the 50-yard line. Then, on second down and 7, he threw a long pass. It was miraculously intercepted by Billy, who, with the help of some good blocking, carried it all the way back down the field for our first touchdown. Part of my pleasure at having our team score was dampened by Billy's being responsible for it.

Still, it was my chance to kick my first extra point

and tie up the game. I didn't even feel nervous when I ran out, just anxious to see 7 points for us on the scoreboard.

The kick easily cleared the goal posts, and there was a lot of cheering from our side of the stands, but when I ran back to the sidelines everyone was still congratulating Billy and not paying any attention to me at all. Then I immediately had to run back out and kick off again.

Neither team scored again during the first half, and no field goal attempts were even made, so at half time the score was still tied. When the boys ran off the field, I went over to the cheerleaders and asked if they knew where a girls' bathroom was. I was told to follow them, and once inside I splashed a lot of cold water on my face and used the toilet.

The cheerleaders were all very friendly and told me they thought I was doing wonderfully well. They also kept talking about Billy's catch, and I knew if the game had ended right then, Billy would have been the hero of the day. Naturally I would have preferred being the hero, but if it couldn't be me, at least I would have liked it to be Wynn.

When we got back outside, Oak Park's drill team was on the field. I like drill teams about as much as marching bands, which was what came out next. I turned to scan the stands to see if I could find Charles and my family. When I finally located them and waved, they didn't see me. All of them were busy watching some scantily clad baton-twirler.

Half time seemed interminable, but finally it was

over and the rest of the team came out on the field. The second half was far more exciting. Oak Park scored and then we scored and then they scored again. And then we got down to about their 40-yard line. This wasn't really field goal range unless I got off a miraculously good kick, but when the coach called for a time out and motioned me over to him, I thought maybe he was going to try for it.

"Do you know how to pass a ball, Tobey?" he asked me.

This wasn't what I had expected to hear. "Sure," I told him.

"How well?"

I shrugged. "Not as well as I kick, but I can pass okay."

"Listen, Tobey, I've got an idea and I think it can work. Oak Park will never expect you to do anything but punt. What if you were to pass to someone instead of kicking? If we don't get a touchdown out of it, at least we should get a first down. Would you be willing to give it a try?"

I was so excited by the idea I couldn't speak, so just stood there nodding my head up and down. He told me to pass to whoever was open, then sent me into the game.

I was tickled silly by the idea. Instead of just being a kicker, I was also going to get a chance to pass. This would be such a surprise to the other team that I felt sure it would work. It would only work one time, though, because when the other teams in the league heard about it, they'd be watching for me to pass every time I went out to punt.

It was such a great idea, in fact, that I wished I had thought of it myself. But if I had thought of it myself, the coach probably would have discarded the idea. Coaches like to think of things all by themselves.

It didn't work exactly as Coach McKeever had conceived it, but it worked beyond his wildest expectations. Here's what happened.

The center hiked the ball to me, and Oak Park started to drop back for the kick. Then they noticed that all our receivers were heading down the field and that I was standing there getting ready to pass. When this happened, they quickly closed in on the receivers, and I was left standing there, not knowing what to do with the ball because by this time none of my receivers was open. Then inspiration struck, and I tucked the ball under my arm and headed downfield. Any one of their players was big enough to knock me over easily, but I'm a fast runner, and my team, seeing what was happening, started blocking for me as I ran.

It seemed like I was running for miles. I didn't even realize I had scored until I heard all this wild screaming and cheering and a couple of my teammates were hitting me on the back and congratulating me. Usually they hit each other on the rear end, but I guess they thought in my case my back was more appropriate.

I didn't even have time yet to think about what I

had done, as I had to kick the extra point. I did this easily, then headed down the field for the kickoff. I was beginning to feel like a one-man team.

After I had kicked, I headed straight for the coach to apologize for not following his instructions.

He held up his hand for silence when I began to apologize. "I could see you didn't have any receivers open—you did the smart thing. In fact, I was hoping you'd do just that, although I would have kicked myself if you had been hurt."

"I don't get hurt very easily, coach," I told him, which was the truth. As a kid I had fallen off garage roofs and out of trees and never broken anything.

"Well, I'll tell you, Tobey—if you can grow ten inches and gain fifty pounds, I'll consider you for quarterback when you're a senior. You think fast on your feet."

I knew he was just joking with me, but if I could have thought of any way to grow ten inches, I sure would have tried. The fifty pounds would have been easy. I would have just gone to Burger King ten times a day.

I don't know whether my running for a touchdown had demoralized the Oak Park team or what, but they didn't score again in the game. We scored once more, which made the final score Evanston 28, Oak Park 21.

I was pretty nervous about riding home on the bus with the team. The problem was that I had done okay, and I knew some of the team was going to resent that. I didn't think they'd resent my kicking so much, but I didn't think they were probably too thrilled that I had run for a touchdown. It somehow made me look like a show-off. So I asked the coach if it would be all right for me to drive back with my family. He said, sure, so I waited at the bottom of the stands for them to come down. When they saw me, my mom and dad each gave me a big hug, and then Robin, and then I turned to Charles, but all he did was shake my hand. Of course, Charles and I really didn't go in for hugging or emotional displays of any kind. That was something we only tolerated from families.

On the way back, Dad stopped at this restaurant, and we all got steak sandwiches and fries and milk shakes. When I told Dad what the coach had said about my growing ten inches and gaining fifty pounds, he said I could have a banana split for dessert. So Robin and I each had a banana split, and Charles had a double chocolate sundae. I think Mom would have had a banana split, too, if Dad hadn't been along.

We talked about the game the whole time. They were all really proud of me. Robin said she was glad she didn't have to be out there holding the ball in front of all of those people, and Charles said I had shown them that a girl could do anything a boy could do. Then Mom said that was a nice play Billy Rafferty had made, and Charles and I made faces at each other.

"Wynn Neil's really the star of the team," I told my parents, but since he hadn't done anything really spectacular that day, my saying that didn't make much of an impression.

Charles and I had planned on taking a bus to the movies that night, but since we got home pretty late we decided to watch television at his house instead. There was a very good horror movie on that we both wanted to see.

Charles's mom let us make popcorn and take some Cokes down to the basement, so it was just as good as being at a real movie, except we didn't have any chocolate-covered raisins. But what was even better than the movies was that we could talk all we wanted without people telling us to shut up.

I was also afraid that if we went to the movies we'd see a lot of kids there from school, and some of them were sure to make remarks about the game. I think it's fun to perform out on the field, but I'm not very good at accepting compliments. I never know what to say in return. My mother says just to say "thank you" when someone compliments you, but I usually get into an argument instead.

After the movie, we took turns lifting Charles's weights, and while we were doing that, he asked me when I was going to start dating.

"Oh, I don't know," I told him. "Right now I'm in training, so I should probably wait until football season is over." The real truth was that no one had asked me out yet, but he knew that as well as I.

"I'm surprised you're not thinking about going out for the basketball team, too."

"You know I'm too short for basketball."

"You could always try out for the girls' team."

I hadn't thought about that. I'm not so good when I play with the boys, but maybe with the girls . . .

When I got home, Robin was just going to bed. "About a hundred boys have called you tonight, Tobey," she said.

"How many, Robin?"

"Well, maybe one boy a hundred times. I don't know."

"Did he leave his name?"

"No, he just hung up. Mom finally made me leave the phone off the hook."

I had a brief fantasy that it was Wynn calling me, wanting to talk about the game.

Then I had a more realistic fantasy—that it was Billy Rafferty calling, telling me to break a leg. Of the two, that seemed the more likely.

5

Robin woke me up in the morning. "Hey, Tobey, wake up. Wynn Neil's on the phone."

I opened one disbelieving eye. "Are you sure it's Wynn Neil?"

"It's not Billy Rafferty, if that's what you think. I remember his voice."

That was exactly what I thought. Waking me up on a Sunday morning could very well be Billy's idea of torture. But, in case it actually was Wynn Neil, I got up and went downstairs to answer the phone. The only upstairs phone is in my parents' bedroom, and they were still sleeping.

"Hello?"

"Hi, Tobey, how're you doing?"

Miracle of miracles, it was Wynn Neil. "Okay, Wynn. How're you doing?"

"That was a great game you played yesterday, Tobey. I was hoping to be able to talk to you on the ride back, but the coach said you caught a ride with your folks."

I mumbled something noncommittal.

"Listen, Tobey, with you on the team, I think we've really got the season whipped. And I told McKeever that. You were terrific, you know it?"

"Thanks, Wynn, but how do the other guys feel?" Did you hear me, Mom? I actually said thank you to a compliment.

"They're mostly behind you, Tobey. A few that aren't, it's only jealousy. They'd feel the same if you were a guy."

Except for Billy Rafferty, I felt like saying, but I didn't want to ruin a perfectly good conversation with Wynn Neil.

"It was so exciting running for that touchdown," I admitted to him. "I know I'll never get the chance again, but it'll probably be the high point of my career."

He chuckled. "I suppose you know there were scouts from the colleges out there."

"Almost makes me wish I were a boy," I told him. Almost, but not quite. "Do you know who you're going to play for next year?" He was such a good quarterback, I figured he would have his choice.

"I don't plan on playing college ball," he told me.

I was shocked into silence for a moment. "Why not?"

"I'm going to be a doctor—at least I hope so. Anyway, medical school is pretty tough to get into, and I'm going to have to concentrate on my grades."

"You'd rather be a doctor than a football player?"

"Sure would."

"But *why?*" If I were a boy, there would be nothing I'd like more than to play for a pro team when I grew up.

"For one thing, the career lasts longer. And for another, I think it's more important."

I couldn't understand that at all. I'd far rather go to a football game than go to a doctor. "Well, I wish you luck, Wynn. Maybe I'll be coming to you someday when I'm sick."

He chuckled at that. "Incidentally, Tobey, I understand you're going with Charles Staunton. I just wanted to tell you, bring him along to the party if you want."

"I'm not going with him; we're just good friends," I hastened to assure him. Just in case he might have some ideas in that direction himself.

"Well, feel free to invite him if you want."

"Okay, I'll see if he wants to come." Fat chance of ever getting Charles to go to a party.

"Okay, Tobey, I guess I'll see you at practice Monday then."

"See you, Wynn."

"See you, Tobey."

I hung up the phone and looked at the kitchen

clock. Only nine, and I always slept until noon on Sundays.

I went back upstairs and got into bed. Why had Wynn called me? Was he interested in me? Was I interested in him? It didn't really matter. At the moment, all I was interested in was getting some more sleep.

The next time I woke up and went downstairs, my father called to me from the living room. "Hey, Tobey—you're in the *Tribune*."

I would have thought he was kidding me, except I knew the *Chicago Tribune* did give coverage to the high school games. Not a lot, not like they give to the Bears, even though the Bears hardly ever even win, but they always write something.

He held up the paper and I saw there was actually a picture of me running with the ball. It was blurred and you couldn't tell I was a girl, except that under the picture it said, "Suburban Team Employs Female Kicker." I was all set to cut it out of the paper, but my father said to wait until my mother had read that section. I decided I'd start a scrapbook of newspaper clippings.

At breakfast my mother asked me, "Was that you on the phone early this morning?"

"Wynn Neil called her," said Robin.

"That's nice," said my mother.

"He only called to talk about the game," I told her.

I must have sounded as though I were complaining, because my mother said, "Oh, you never know."

"In this case I know, because he happens to be going with the best-looking girl in the school."

"Maybe he feels he has more in common with you," said my mother. My mother is very big on having things in common with people. She is always telling people how much she and my father have in common.

I didn't argue with her, though, because I wanted to believe that maybe she was right. My fantasies about football were turning into fantasies about football *and* Wynn . . . and sometimes *just* Wynn. I didn't really think I had a chance with Wynn, but then I hadn't thought I had a chance of getting on the team, either, and since one of my fantasies had come true, why not all of them? Maybe it was going to be my lucky year and I'd get everything I wanted. Then again, maybe it wasn't.

After breakfast I talked Robin into going outside with me while I practiced. Behind our fenced-in backyard we have a lot that goes all the way out to the alley. It's full of weeds and stuff, but I've cleared off most of it so that I can use it. I not only wanted to practice kicking, I'd also decided to practice some passing just in case the coach asked me to pass the ball again. I really didn't think that would happen, but I wanted to be prepared just in case.

The only problem was Robin couldn't catch the ball. I would tell her to run out, and then I would throw the ball, but it was hard to tell whether my passes were on the mark, because she never ended up catching any of them.

We had been out there about an hour—and I could tell Robin would have preferred to be doing something else—when Wynn Neil came up behind me. When I saw him there, I almost fainted dead away from shock.

"Your dad said you were back here," he told me, watching as Robin again missed a pass. "What are you doing, practicing to take over my job?"

"I couldn't do that if I wanted to," I said to him, but then he just laughed, so I guessed he was kidding.

"I think it's a pretty good idea for you to practice passing. We ought to be able to pull that a couple more times this season, and you might as well be ready. Want me to show you how?"

Of course I wanted him to show me how. I would have been glad for Wynn to show me how to do anything. I was kind of sorry I hadn't even combed my hair, but he didn't seem to be noticing.

I told Robin she didn't have to catch the ball anymore, and she looked kind of knowingly at me and Wynn before going back in the house.

First he showed me how to run patterns, then he passed the ball to me for a while. Then we switched places and I passed the ball to him. Then Wynn found a stick and a patch of dirt, and we sat on the ground while he diagrammed some plays for me. They were the same plays Coach McKeever had diagrammed on the blackboard, but this time I felt free to ask questions. I hadn't wanted to appear dumb in front of the other boys. I thought it was really nice for Wynn to go to all this trouble for me.

He was really treating me like an equal. Other than Charles, no one else treated me that way.

After we had been out there for about an hour and a half, he asked me if I wanted to go for a ride. I told him sure and that I'd just let my parents know where I was going. Then I went into the house and washed the dirt off my hands and face and combed my hair. My mother gave me that knowing look again when I told her where I was going. I was beginning to think Robin and Mom, with their knowing looks, maybe knew more than I did.

I felt really strange to be getting into the front seat of Wynn's car. This wasn't like driving home from football practice; it was really something like a date—or at least like what a boy does when he likes a girl. I was kind of hoping Charles would see me and also kind of hoping he wouldn't. I was sure that he hadn't believed for a moment that some boy would actually ask me out. Of course Wynn *hadn't* asked me out yet, but this seemed pretty close.

First he drove up to Wilmette to a drive-in I'd never been to, and we ordered Cokes. I figured we were up there because he didn't want anyone he knew to see me with him. We were sitting there talking about the game when these two really cute guys came over to the car and said, "Hey, Wynn."

Wynn introduced me to them, and they turned out to be two of New Trier's players. We were playing them next week. They started to kid him about hearing we had a girl on the team.

"I'll bet she looks like a moose, right?" said one

of the guys. "We've seen some of those tough Evanston girls."

I had to laugh when they said that, and Wynn was laughing, too. Then he told them *I* was the girl, and they looked really surprised.

"Hey, you can play on our team anytime," one of them said to me, and the other one was really looking me over.

"You guys should get with the times and have your own girl on the team," Wynn told them, and I could see they didn't think that was such a bad idea.

"See you next week, Wynn," they said, and then they both stuck their heads in the window and said how they were really looking forward to seeing me next week.

Then Wynn got out of the car and walked them over to their car, and they stood there talking a few minutes. When he came back, he said, "They wanted your phone number, but I didn't give it to them."

"How come?" I asked.

"How come I didn't give it to them?"

"No, how come they wanted it?"

He smiled and said, "Why do you think boys want girls' telephone numbers?"

"Oh." It was surprising what playing football seemed to be doing for my social life. I wouldn't have minded going out with either one of them, but I suspected my parents would prefer me sticking to boys from my own school.

Even though New Trier doesn't have such a good football team, they're our biggest rivals, because their school is the closest to ours. And their other teams are good. They nearly always beat us in basketball, and their swimming team is rated number one in the state. We figure that their football team isn't so good because the kids who go to New Trier are richer than we are, and therefore not so tough. This is just an assumption, though, and may not be true.

Wynn was watching me, and it was making me nervous. "I wouldn't have wanted Charles to get mad at me for giving out your phone number," he finally said.

"I told you, Charles and I are just good friends. Actually, he's my best friend."

"I know that's what you say, but that's what movie stars always say about someone, and then the next week you read about them getting married."

"Well, Charles and I aren't getting married!"

"Not yet, anyway."

"Don't you believe girls and boys can be friends?" I asked him.

"I guess I really don't believe that. I've never had a girl for a friend."

I was sorry to hear that, as I was hoping he was thinking of me as a friend. But then if he wasn't thinking of me as a friend, maybe he was thinking of me as something more. And that would even be better.

I got up my nerve and said, "Aren't you and Suzanna friends?"

He laughed. "That's a little different, Tobey."

"How is it different?"

"It just is, believe me. Anyway, Suzanna and I aren't going steady anymore."

This was news to me. Big news! "You aren't?"

"Do you think I'd be here with you if we were?"

"I hadn't thought about it. I just figured maybe since we're teammates . . ."

"I'm still seeing her, but we decided that since we'll be going away to different colleges next year, we should start dating other people—not get so serious."

"And are you dating other people?" I figured that since he had been the one to bring it up, it was all right to ask questions.

"She's been going out with some guy from Northwestern."

He didn't say he was dating anyone else, so I thought maybe I'd better drop it. Anyhow, if he was, I really didn't want to hear about it.

He pulled out of the drive-in then and headed back towards Evanston. He changed the subject and started telling me about New Trier's team. I didn't pay a whole lot of attention. I was still thinking about the fact that he wasn't going steady anymore. I still couldn't believe he could possibly be interested in me. You just didn't go from dating the prettiest girl in the school to seeing me. That just didn't make sense.

When he pulled up in front of my house, he cut his motor and didn't seem in a hurry to leave. I wasn't in a hurry, either, even though I knew dinner was probably ready.

"Do you want to go by school and get in a little practice?"

"You practice at school on Sunday?"

"Nothing official. We just get together, and the defense plays the offense."

"I don't think the other boys would appreciate that."

"Come on. I'll even let you be quarterback."

That was too tempting to resist. "Okay, but just let me go inside and tell my folks."

"But dinner's ready, Tobey," said my mother.

"Oh please, Mom," I begged. "Just this once."

She raised one of her eyebrows. "Are you getting serious about this boy?"

"No! I'm serious about football!"

She seemed to relent. "All right, but why don't you take some chicken with you to eat in the car?"

I didn't mind that idea at all, so she wrapped some up and put in some paper napkins, and when I got back to the car, Wynn and I sat there and ate it. Then we went to another drive-in and got two more Cokes to wash it down. Then we drove to the high school.

Practically the whole team was there playing a game of tackle in just their jeans and t-shirts. Billy Rafferty was one of them, and he didn't look pleased to see me show up. He gave Wynn a look as though he thought Wynn was mentally retarded just to be with me.

Nobody on the offense team argued with Wynn when he told them I was going to be quarterback, but nobody exactly cheered, either. The only problem was I didn't know any of the plays, so when we went into a huddle I just made one up. I simply told them I was going to pass the ball and for all the receivers to be ready.

The defense wasn't expecting a pass, since none of them even knew I *could* pass, so I threw it successfully to Bill Bowers and he ran for another first down.

The next time I wasn't so successful. I felt like passing again, but this time they were expecting it and I got sacked. What that means is one guy tackled me, and then about six more piled up on top of us.

And naturally the one who tackled me was mean Billy Rafferty. There he was, right on top of me, his face only about a half inch from my own. I could even feel his warm breath and tell that he had recently eaten onions. I think I must have gotten the breath knocked out of me, because I got a funny feeling in my stomach.

Billy was right over me glaring at me and I finally said, "All right, will you just get off of me?"

And then Wynn came by and said, "Come on, guys, let's not injure our kicker."

The other guys got up, and then Billy reluctantly got up. "If she wants to play with the big boys she's got to take her chances," he said with a scowl.

"If she gets hurt, it hurts the whole team," Wynn told him, but Billy didn't look convinced.

I didn't need Wynn protecting me—I could take care of myself.

On the next play, I passed the ball off and we didn't get anywhere. So then we punted and the other team had the ball. I was determined to get even with Billy, so when I saw him take off as though he was going to be passed the ball, I ran right after him, keeping next to him the whole time. Then, when he attempted to catch the ball, I threw all my weight against him, hoping to drive him into the ground.

It didn't quite work out that way. My block hardly even fazed him, but it really hurt my shoulder, and I was the one to fall to the ground. Billy just caught the ball and ran for a touchdown.

"You okay, Tobey?" Wynn asked me.

"I think I broke my shoulder."

He smiled. "If you had broken your shoulder, you'd be screaming now. And, by the way, you can't hit the receiver like that—that's interference."

I had known that but was hoping they'd think I didn't know any better and let me get away with it.

Wynn reached his hand down and helped me up. My shoulder was sore all right, but it didn't seem to be broken, and when he asked if I wanted to just watch for a while, I said no, I wanted to play.

"Nice try," Billy said to me sarcastically. "I almost felt it."

I muttered something under my breath. It was just as well nobody heard.

"I wouldn't advise you to go out for tackle," Billy went on, getting a big laugh from the guys.

"Shut up, Rafferty," I said, but he just laughed.

The rest of the game I stayed out of Billy's way and he stayed out of mine. It was a lot of fun being the quarterback, much more interesting than just being the kicker and, not for the first time, I found myself thinking that being a boy had its advantages.

Wynn drove a couple of the other guys home, but he dropped them off first. When he got to my house, he parked with the motor running. Then, when I turned to thank him for everything, he leaned over and kissed me on the mouth. He did it so fast I didn't even know what was happening at first; then I was so surprised I didn't even move away. He didn't put his arm around me or anything —just put his mouth on top of mine and gave me about a ten-second kiss, my very first kiss since the fifth grade, when we used to play spin-the-bottle at birthday parties.

"What was that for?" I asked stupidly when he stopped kissing me.

He looked amused. "I just felt like it, that's all."

I didn't know what to say to that, so I got out of the car and watched as he drove off. I was hoping like crazy that no one had been watching out of a window.

He must like me, I was thinking to myself. He wouldn't kiss me if he didn't like me, would he?

And then I was sorry I hadn't concentrated more on the kiss, because already I could hardly remember what it was like. I couldn't even remember if I had kissed him back. I wasn't even sure I knew *how* to kiss someone back. I was just glad he hadn't opened his mouth when he kissed me. I hear some of the boys do that, but it sounds pretty gross to me. I supposed Billy Rafferty kissed like that.

When I got into the house, everyone was watching television, so I told them I was home, then I went across the street to see Charles. This was the first Sunday in a long time that I hadn't spent with him, and I was hoping he wouldn't be mad.

Ten minutes later Charles was saying, "I'm not kissing you, Tobey—you can just forget it!"

"Come on, it's just an experiment."

"Then experiment on someone else." He was circling around the room, trying to get out of my reach.

I had thought it would be a good idea for Charles to kiss me so that I could compare it with Wynn's kiss. I didn't know what to think of Wynn's kiss unless I compared it with someone else's.

"What's the big deal, Charles? You've got to kiss a girl sometime."

"But not now!"

"What good are you as a best friend if you won't even do me one little favor." I cornered him and he was looking like a scared rabbit.

"If I was your best friend and a girl, you wouldn't ask me to be doing this."

"But you're not a girl, and the least you can do is help me with an experiment. You're the one who goes in for experiments, Charles. Just consider this scientific research."

"You're making me feel really stupid!"

"That's because you're acting stupid. It's only a kiss, Charles, one lousy kiss."

"Oh, sure. Now that you've been kissed once, you act like it's nothing. Maybe I want it to mean something the first time I kiss a girl—did you ever think of that?"

"You said you'd date me if I wanted to date. If we dated, you'd have to kiss me."

"Who says?"

"*I* do."

"Maybe if I ever do kiss you, I won't want it to be an experiment. Maybe I don't like being compared to Wynn Neil, did you ever think of that?"

I stood back from him in surprise. "You're not jealous of Wynn, are you?" How could a person be jealous when his best friend got kissed?

"No, I'm not jealous," he said, but his voice was gruff and he wasn't looking very happy.

I moved back in on him. "Come on, Charles, just one kiss; it's not going to kill you."

And then I leaned real close to him and put my mouth right next to his. I didn't think he'd really do it, but suddenly he was kissing me. I started counting off the seconds, and when I got to ten I broke it off.

"See? You're still in one piece," I told him, going over to the television and turning it on.

"That's all you can say?"

"What do you want me to say?"

"What are you going to do, Tobey—go around kissing all the boys in the school and comparing them? Maybe you could give out gold stars or something."

"Very funny, Charles."

"Well?"

"Well, what?"

"Well, how did I compare?"

"What do you want, a gold star, Charles?"

He stormed across the room and lay down on his bed. I could tell he was about to go into one of his sulks.

"Listen, Charles, if you want to know the truth, you kiss just as well as Wynn Neil, and he's the most popular boy in the school."

I figured that would make him feel better, but he didn't say anything.

"Honest, Charles—I'm not kidding."

He still didn't say anything, so I shrugged and gave a loud sigh, then told him I'd see him in the morning. I expected him to tell me to stay, but he didn't say anything, so I went home. I would just as soon watch television with my family as with Charles when he's sulking. I bet Wynn Neil doesn't sulk!

But instead of watching television, I decided it wouldn't be a bad idea to do my homework, which up until then I had conveniently forgotten. This took about two hours, and then I got ready for bed. What I really wanted was some quiet time in bed to think about Wynn Neil.

I was just starting to seriously think when Robin knocked on my door. I told her she could come in.

"Is Wynn Neil your boyfriend now?" she asked me.

"Don't be silly."

"Well, he called you up and came over to see you and then took you for a ride. If a boy did that with me, I'd think he was my boyfriend."

I felt like telling her he'd also kissed me, but decided not to. She might tell my folks, and then I'd really be embarrassed.

"We're just football buddies."

"But you like him, don't you?"

"Sure I like him."

"Better than Charles?"

"Charles is my best friend."

Charles being my best friend seemed endlessly confusing to her. She felt only girls could be other girls' best friends.

"Okay, Tobey, good night," she said, closing my door.

What was bothering me about Wynn's kiss was the fact that I couldn't remember being thrilled by it. I hadn't been expecting fireworks to go off or the earth to move, but I was expecting to feel something. As it was, it hadn't felt any different to me than Charles's kiss—except with Charles it hadn't

98

been as unexpected, since I had practically forced him to kiss me.

But maybe kissing was something you had to learn to enjoy, like beer. My father drinks a lot of beer. He lets me taste it, but I always make faces. He says he didn't like it at first either, but after you get used to it, it tastes really good. Maybe kissing's like that.

I just hope I get a chance to find out.

6

It is rather tiring to be an instant celebrity. If I counted all the people who said hello to me at school on Monday, I would have thought I was the most popular girl in school. Starting with home room, where, after other announcements, my home room teacher mentioned me being in the game on Saturday, and everyone applauded me—it went on like that all day. Except for girls' chorus—I don't think our singing teacher, Ms. Manfredi, knows what football is—every other teacher I had mentioned it, too, and all the kids would turn to look at me.

All day in the halls kids I knew and kids I didn't know would come up to me and say, "Good game on Saturday, Tobey," or something about like that.

In the cafeteria, the football players banged their trays against the table as I walked by—Billy Rafferty was notably absent, thank goodness—and at practically every other table I passed I was forced to stop and say a few words. I didn't have to stop at Katie Lou Slight's table, and I could see her looking absolutely furious as I passed by. Some of her friends sneaked smiles at me, though, and I was wondering if she was losing some of her influence. There was a time when none of them would smile without Katie Lou smiling first.

The cheerleaders looked welcoming and so I sat with them again, but they weren't any substitute for Charles. I had had a lot more fun eating lunch with him last year.

I was just starting to eat my lettuce sandwich when Coleman Brown came up to me and said he had gotten Coach McKeever's permission to interview me for the school paper. He asked if he could sit down. I would have preferred being interviewed in privacy, but the cheerleaders made a big fuss about it, so I told him okay. He asked me a lot of questions he read out of his notebook, and wrote down all my answers. I answered all of them truthfully, except for the one about what did I think of cheerleaders. I couldn't very well tell him what I really thought, since they were sitting right there and could hear everything I said. Anyway, they were pretty nice girls, and I didn't feel the way about cheerleaders that I had previously, particularly since I had found out two of them were on the school swimming team and one on the tennis team. Prior to that I had thought all they did was cheer and comb their hair.

Charles had acted all right on the school bus that morning and I guess you could say he acted all right in geometry, but he wasn't acting the way he usually acted. I think he was still miffed at me for making him kiss me. I was thinking that maybe when I got Wynn Neil all wrapped up (this was positive thinking on my part, not certainty) I would try to find him a girlfriend. I was sure almost any freshman girl would be happy to have him for a boyfriend; I wasn't so sure about the sophomore girls, who usually prefer dating older guys.

I wrote him a note telling him that Wynn Neil had said he could come to the party on Saturday night—I had forgotten to tell him before. He handed the note back to me with "No thanks!" written on the bottom. I thought he was missing a very good opportunity to have a social life, but I was also secretly relieved, as I wasn't sure I wanted Charles to see me with Wynn Neil.

As I was heading out to the field for football practice that day, Billy Rafferty and three of his friends surrounded me. One of them came up behind me and put his hand over my eyes. Then, before I could fight him off, someone else held the neck of my football jersey out and dropped something down inside my shirt. Whatever it was couldn't fall out, because my shirt was tucked into my pants.

When the hand was taken off my eyes, Billy was

standing in front of me, a big evil grin on his hateful face.

I stood very still as I looked down and saw something moving around inside my shirt. I knew those boys were just waiting for me to start screaming and jumping around and carrying on, but they had picked the wrong victim. I pulled the front of my shirt out and looked down. There was a garter snake trapped inside my shirt.

Now, if there's one thing I'm not afraid of, it's garter snakes. When I was a kid and neighbors used to find them and cut them in half and throw them out in the street, I used to retrieve them and tape them back together. Then, when they finally died, I'd give them a decent burial out in the vacant lot behind my house. I would sometimes even bury treasure with them. They are harmless little snakes, and there's no reason to be afraid of them at all. Billy had picked his object of terror poorly—if he had put a spider down my neck, he would have seen more action.

I pulled my shirt out of my pants, holding my hand to catch the snake when it fell out. Then I walked over to a grassy area and let the snake loose. All this time I hadn't said a word to Billy Rafferty, just ignored him as Charles had suggested I do. And Charles was right—it worked. Not getting the reaction they had looked for, Billy and his friends finally just slunk off to practice.

Along with kicking, the coach also let me practice throwing the ball that day. I think he knew something was going on between me and Billy, because he made Billy act as my receiver. Billy mumbled something about not wanting to have to catch for a girl, but the coach told him if he saw him miss any, he'd have to do extra practice. I could see Billy was wishing I had never been born. Well, the feeling was mutual!

For about an hour I had to pass the ball while Billy ran out to receive it. I cheated and tried to throw it too far so that he'd miss it, but he always managed to make the extra effort, and the result was some spectacular catches. The coach finally noticed and came over and congratulated us.

"You two make a dynamite combination," he told us, obviously thinking we were going to be pleased by the compliment.

Both of us just grumbled and were relieved to be able to go off and practice something else. Afterwards in the gym the coach said he was going to use me in the game next Saturday to pass, if the opportunity came up. He diagrammed a few plays for me, and this time I felt free to ask questions. He also told me, though, that he didn't want me running with the ball.

"You're fast, Tobey, but I don't want to risk your getting injured."

Well, fun as it was, I didn't want to risk injury, either. It was enough to know that I had done it once.

We were all pretty happy that week. We had beaten the toughest team in the league, and the game with New Trier should be a snap. I was also glad it was a home game, as a lot more kids from school would get to see me play. Well, I did say I was a show-off, didn't I?

That night after dinner I went across the street to see Charles.

"You've got to help me think of an idea to get Billy Rafferty," I told him. "Today he put a snake down my shirt."

I could see that Charles was trying not to laugh. But that was okay, 'cause he knows I'm not afraid of snakes.

"Why don't you put a Kenny doll down *his* shirt?"

"I'd like to put a bomb down his shirt!"

Charles's eyes lit up. "I could make a stink bomb for you, and you could put it in his car."

For about ten seconds I thought that was a great idea. Then reason took over. "No, if I do something like that, he'll just retaliate with something worse. I have to do something that will either humiliate him in front of his friends or threaten him in some way so that he's afraid to retaliate."

Charles shrugged. "The only thing that seems to bother him is mention of his Kenny doll."

"I have a feeling that half the boys on the team probably had dolls of some kind when they were young. They'd probably all stick together."

"Probably even Wynn Neil."

I gave Charles a warning look.

"Okay, Tobey, but what do you think would embarrass him?"

I couldn't think of a thing. "I don't think there's

anything that would embarrass him. He's really too gross to be embarrassed."

"He really hates you, doesn't he?"

I nodded. "The feeling is mutual."

"Then that's what would embarrass him."

I must have missed something there. "What are you talking about, Charles?"

"Make everyone think he likes you. I'll bet that'll make him leave you alone."

"How can I make everyone think he likes me when everyone knows he hates me."

Charles had on his clever, devious face. "You could do it, Tobey. Just say things in front of his friends like, 'Oh, Billy, that was so sweet of you to call last night,' or 'Billy, darling, are you coming over to see me again?'"

"I don't say stuff like that, Charles."

"I know you don't, but you could."

Sure I could, and then Wynn Neil would hear me and that would be the end of that. "I don't want the whole school to think I'm going with Billy Rafferty," I protested.

"You mean you don't want Wynn Neil to think so." Charles is no slouch when it comes to figuring things out.

I didn't admit it or deny it.

"Look, Tobey, couldn't you tell Wynn what you plan on doing? He's on your side, isn't he?"

I grinned at him. "Charles, you're a genius."

He shrugged. "Of course."

I asked him if I could use his phone, and when he said yes, I called information and got Wynn's number. When I called, Wynn answered, which was quite a relief. If someone else had answered, I probably would have chickened out and hung up.

"Hi, Wynn—it's Tobey."

"Hey, Tobey—how're ya doing?"

"Great. Listen, Wynn, will you do me a favor?"

"Sure, if I can."

"I just want to tell you to ignore anything you hear me say about or to Billy Rafferty the rest of the week. It won't be true, okay?"

"Whatever you say, Tobey."

"I've just got a little plan to get even with him, that's all."

"You need any help?"

"Thanks, but I don't think so. I just didn't want you to think any of it was true."

"Okay, Tobey."

"Thanks, Wynn. I have to hang up now. I'm over at Charles's house."

"See you tomorrow, Tobey."

I gave Charles a big grin and we shook hands. "Tomorrow at this time the enemy should be neutralized."

The next day I could hardly wait until my first encounter with Billy Rafferty. This took place sooner than expected, because he was in the cafeteria during my lunch hour again. I wasn't sure I'd have the nerve to say something with so many kids around—at football practice would have been easier—but when I passed by his table, I just couldn't resist the temptation.

"Hi, Billy," I said to him, just as sweet as could be. "Did you finally get to sleep last night?"

And while he was sitting there looking very confused, as well he might, and his friends were looking from him to me, I went on down the aisle and sat with the cheerleaders.

"I see you're thinking better of Billy these days," Karen said to me.

Feeling like an utter fool, I said, "Oh, Billy's really a sweetie."

I never said anything like that before in my whole life, and I was afraid they'd laugh at me. But since they all talk like that, they didn't seem to notice anything unusual about it. I could see the cafeteria was kind of buzzing about it. Well, I could hardly blame them. The time before I had dumped chocolate milk over his head.

I couldn't wait to tell Charles in geometry. We spent the whole period passing notes back and forth about what I would say to Billy at football practice.

I ran out to football practice with even more enthusiasm than usual. Being wicked is really a lot of fun. If Billy thought a snake was bad, wait until he saw what I had up my sleeve.

I ran right over to where he was standing around with his friends, and I looked up at him with great big eyes. I've seen girls do this with boys, and it always seems effective. Of course, that's because most boys are so dumb. I was counting on Billy to be just as dumb.

"Billy, honey, are we going to get to play catch

together again today?" I asked him in this sickeningly sweet voice.

Billy wasn't as dumb as I had counted on. His eyes narrowed, and he grabbed me by the arm and pulled me off to the side away from his friends, who were now all snickering.

"What are you trying to pull, Tyler?" he hissed at me.

I leaned against him so that his friends could see the action but not hear the words. "Just a little warning, Rafferty," I said softly. Then, in an extra loud voice, I said, "Oh, Billy, do you really mean that?"

Billy turned a gratifying shade of red. "I dare you to try this in private with me," he said, his eyes looking dangerous.

I giggled girlishly. If this sounds sickening, it's because it was. "We'll have all the privacy you want when you come over tonight," I said, again loudly.

"If you think you're going to get away with this—"

"I think I already have, Rafferty," I said quietly, then turned and walked off, stopping for just a moment to wave him a cute little good-bye.

I went over to where Wynn, convulsed in laughter, was standing with the coach. "Do I get to practice with Billy again, coach?" I asked him.

"Later, Tobey. Go practice your kicking with Ted for a while."

I saw Wynn wink at me as I went off, and I winked back. I was glad to see he remembered what I said and wasn't taking it seriously. Although I didn't see how anyone could take it seriously, not considering the way Billy and I always got along.

I practiced my kicking, but my mind wasn't on it. I was rehearsing what I'd say when the chance came to throw Billy the ball. I wanted to drive him absolutely insane, so that he'd be begging for a truce. And yet I wasn't even sure I wanted a truce. Now that I seemed to be getting the upper hand, I was enjoying it immensely.

After what seemed like hours, the coach finally told me and Billy to practice together. We went over to the other side of the field by ourselves, and I could tell Billy wasn't looking forward to it. Poor thing, I almost took pity on him for a moment. But then I remembered how evil he really was.

I made all these beautiful long passes, and every time he went to catch one, I would call out something like, "That's the way, Billy, honey," or "I know you can do it, darling," and Billy was so flustered he missed half the catches. He was stumbling over his big feet in frustration, and every time he missed I called out, "Oh, too bad, honey," or something to that effect. Everyone could hear us and the other guys were laughing so hard the practice was practically a shambles. I was just afraid the coach might say something to me like I should keep my private life out of the practice. Wynn told me later, though, that he had told the coach what was going on, and the coach thought it was pretty funny.

What happened in the parking lot later wasn't so funny. I came out of the school and headed for Wynn's car. I saw he was already in it, but I also saw Billy leaning against his, his friends kind of standing around in between. It looked like a trap, but I couldn't figure out what kind. I wasn't afraid, though, not with Wynn right there.

I decided it wasn't the right time to tease Billy anymore that day, so I just headed for the other side of Wynn's car to get in. Billy's low voice stopped me.

"Aren't you driving home with me . . . darling?" His mouth was smiling, but his eyes looked mean.

I didn't know whether to keep faking it or not, and then Wynn said, "Come on, Tobey, get in the car."

I reached for the door handle, and Billy's voice stopped me again.

"What's the matter, honey, you chicken?"

Billy knew very well how I felt about dares. He should—he had dared me to do enough things when we were kids. He knew I just couldn't stand to turn down a dare.

"No, I'm not chicken, Rafferty."

His smile widened. "Then let's go, honey. Let's get some of that privacy you were talking about before."

His friends were hanging on to every word as though this were the surprise ending to a movie.

"Tobey!" Wynn's voice came like a warning.

I looked at Wynn, then back at Billy.

He was nodding. "Do I have to say I dare you?"

I stuck out my lower lip and marched over to his car. He even opened the door for me, rather in the manner of a spider luring a fly.

"Do you want me to follow you, Tobey?" asked Wynn.

But Billy's friends were still watching, and I wanted to really cook his goose with them.

"No thanks, Wynn—Billy and I want to be alone."

Billy heard that as he got in his side of the car, and I could hear him chuckle. "You're more of a fool than I thought," he said, sounding mysterious.

His car didn't have bucket seats and I sat over as close to the door as I could get, my arm and head practically out the window. He started up the car and moved fast out of the parking lot, then made a turn in the exact opposite direction of where we lived.

As he drove, he rested his right arm along the back of the seat. "Why don't you move over here and be friendly, Tobey?"

"Why don't you get stuffed?"

His hand started to play with my hair, and I leaned forward out of his reach. "Is that any way to talk to me? What happened to 'darling'? And 'honey'?"

"Just shut up, Billy, and drive me home!"

"I don't think so, Tobey. I think like you said, we nt to be alone."

"You try anything, Billy, and I'm jumping out of this car."

"You would, too, wouldn't you? You know something, Tobey? I think you must be the most annoying girl in the whole school."

"Wynn doesn't find me annoying."

He laughed. "Wynn feels girls need protecting."

"I don't need any protecting!"

"Let's see if you feel that way twenty minutes from now."

"Is that a threat, Rafferty?"

"Would I threaten you?"

He was heading in the direction of Lake Michigan, which was not on the way home. If worse came to worse, I figured I could always get out of the car and make a run for it. If possible, though, I wanted to win this skirmish. I had had the upper hand with him today, and I didn't want to lose it. Anyway, I didn't think Billy Rafferty would dare to do anything bad to me. He was probably a coward when his friends weren't around.

Except he wasn't acting like a coward. He was acting as though he had everything under control. He was a good driver, too.

"If I'm so annoying, Rafferty, why don't you just let me out? I can take a bus home."

"I find you a challenge."

Oh, great! Maybe he was going to challenge me to a duel down on the beach. Or arm wrestling, although it had been years since I was able to beat him at that. And the only time I did beat him it was because I managed to twist his thumb really far back and caught him unawares.

"If you want to call a truce, Billy . . ."

"I'm not interested in a truce. I'm interested in winning."

"What's winning, getting me off the team? I'll fight you to the death before I'll drop off the team, Billy—I love it."

"Why would I want you off the team? Then we couldn't have these sweet moments together."

I felt like making a barfing noise, but then decided it was beneath my dignity. "You make me sick, Billy Rafferty!"

"You prefer a gentleman like Wynn Neil, right? Or Charles?" He sounded amused, like he knew something I didn't.

"I prefer anyone to you."

"Anyone?"

"I prefer that snake you put down my neck. You're worse than a snake, you know that?"

He laughed. "I should have remembered about you and snakes. You remember the time you tied me to the tree and were going to apply Indian torture?"

That had been when I was about seven and Billy was eight. It took three of us to capture him and tie him up, then I went into my house and got some honey and put it all over his bare feet. It was supposed to attract ants, and the ants were supposed to eat him up, but all it attracted were some flies and they only tickled him. Which reminded me—Billy was ticklish. If he tried anything, I'd just start tickling him. I could do it now, but I didn't want him to lose control of the car.

"I remember. I should never have untied you."

"You didn't. You left me there and my sisters finally found me."

I looked over at him. "And now you're getting even with me?" He sure had a long memory.

"I think I got even with you that time I dared you to climb to the top of the tree and the fire department had to come to get you down."

"I could've gotten down myself."

"As I recall, you were screaming bloody murder."

"I was screaming for your blood, not to be gotten down."

"You remember the time we were running under your sprinklers and we decided to take all our clothes off?"

"Never mind, Billy!" We had only been about five and six, but I still didn't feel like reminiscing about it.

"What's the matter, Tobey?" His voice was a soft drawl.

"Yes, we had a lot of fun when we were children. Now, why don't we go home?"

"Don't you think we should relive our happy childhoods? Go down to the beach, throw off all our clothes, and go running through the waves?"

"You have the dirtiest mind of any boy I know, Billy Rafferty!"

"*Me?* I'm just thinking about getting wet. You better examine your own mind, Tobey."

I was so furious I could barely speak. "What happy childhoods? As I recall, all we ever did was fight. Rather like now, as a matter of fact."

He looked over at me. "You're cute when you're mad."

"You're going to be sorry for this."

"Am I?"

He could be so infuriating! "Remember when we used to play dolls, Billy? I bet you still have your Kenny doll somewhere, don't you?"

"It's not going to work, Tobey. The only dolls I play with these days are alive and preferably blond."

"I'm not a blonde," I told him.

"Sure you are."

He was pulling into a parking lot overlooking the lake. The place was deserted, unfortunately. He pulled into one of the parking places and cut his motor. Then he turned towards me and said, "You want to play?"

I got out of the car and started running in the direction of the beach. There were some narrow, steep stone steps leading down to the sand that slowed me down, but I figured they'd slow him down, too. I had probably chosen the wrong direction to run. If I had headed for the street there would probably have been other people around and he wouldn't dare stop me, but there was no one on the beach at that hour. Which reminded me, I'd probably be late getting home to dinner.

Once I hit the sand I looked back and saw him halfway down the stairs. I started running north along the beach, my feet hardly touching the ground. I was much lighter than he was and thought I could run faster, but his longer legs made up for the weight difference. I looked back and saw him gaining on me, and I didn't see what good running was going to do anymore, because there was nowhere to run to, only more and more beach stretching for miles.

Then he made a lunge and tackled me, sending us both sprawling in the sand. Getting tackled in the sand doesn't hurt the way it does on the hard ground, but I still didn't appreciate getting sand all over my face and in my hair. Now I'd have to wash it again.

He sat up cross-legged and looked over at me. "You ever think of going out for track?"

This was so unexpected I could only gape. I thought he'd say something about having won again.

"You're fast—you ought to think about it."

I sat up, brushing the sand off my face and shaking out my hair. "Yeah, well, maybe I will."

"You're good. You might even get a college scholarship for track. You won't get one for football, you know."

"I know." What was he trying to do, lull me with all this mundane talk?

He stood up and reached out his hand for me, but I got up on my own.

"Come on, I'll take you home." He said it quietly, and it was so unexpected that I followed him silently to the car. I don't know what I had expected, but it wasn't that he'd suddenly start acting like a gentleman. It didn't fit him, somehow, and I was almost disappointed.

He didn't even try to make me mad all the way home. He didn't say anything, just turned on the radio to a rock station and drove fast, which was fine with me as I was already late and didn't want to have to explain to my parents that the reason for my lateness was because Billy Rafferty had been chasing me down a deserted beach.

When he pulled up in front of my house and I started to get out, he said, "I hope I didn't scare you, Tobey."

"You? Don't be silly," I told him, and I could hear his laugh as he drove off.

For some reason it seemed like a very boring end to what had been, in retrospect, one of my more exciting experiences.

7

On Wednesday my interview came out in the school paper. I'd rather just forget it ever happened, but since some people are making it impossible for me to forget, this is it in its entirety:

This is Coleman Brown, interviewing Ms. Tobey Tyler, the first girl in Evanston's history to have a starting position on the varsity football team.

Q: How does it feel, Tobey, to be the first girl to play on our football team?
A: It feels great. I wish now I had tried out last year.
Q: Do you think more girls should try out for the team?

A: Yes, I definitely do. In fact I can see, maybe a few years from now, football teams made up of mostly girls.

Q: Mostly girls? Why is that?

A: It's mainly a matter of intelligence, Coleman. We all know girls are more intelligent than boys, and football is a game that requires intelligence. Girls are also faster than boys. Now I know that some positions, like tackle, are better played by boys, because all that's required of a tackle is that he be big. He doesn't have to have any intelligence at all. And I think girls could get big with the proper diet and exercise. If you just think about the women athletes in Russia, you'll see what I mean.

Q: I take it what you're saying, Tobey, is that boys are stupid.

A: Not all boys, Coleman. I'm sure that you're intelligent, and I know of one or two others who are. But for the most part the girls seem to have cornered the market on intelligence.

Q: What about Evanston's football team. Would you say it's an intelligent team?

A: Now you're putting me on the spot. Let me just say we have an intelligent coaching staff and intelligent boys in the positions that require intelligence.

Q: Let's be more specific, Tobey. Would you characterize any players on the team as stupid?

A: (Long pause) I don't think you really want me to answer that, Coleman.

Q: On the contrary, Tobey, not only would I like to hear your answer, but I'm sure all our readers would be interested.

A: Well, I would say that there's at least one I wouldn't call bright.

Q: There have been rumors circulating around school about a "chocolate milk" incident. Would you like to elaborate on that?

A: No.

Q: I understand it involved a football player.

A: I'd really rather not comment on that, Coleman.

Q: Just off the record, Tobey, would you say that that incident involved a "not so bright" player?

A: This is off the record?

Q: Right.

A: Yes, he's probably the stupidest boy in the whole entire world.

Q: Thank you for being candid, Tobey. How about cheerleaders? Would you characterize them as intelligent?

A: They're girls, aren't they?

Q: Back to football. How do you think our team will do this season?

A: I think we're unbeatable.

Q: You envision going to the playoffs?

A: I not only envision it, I look forward to it.

Q: Let me say I wish you great success this first year of yours on the team, Tobey, and I want to thank you for this controversial interview.

A: Controversial?

This is Coleman Brown, saying one of the other football players will be given equal time in next week's issue in order to answer some of the allegations posed by Tobey Tyler.

The paper came out on Wednesday morning. I didn't see a copy of it until after lunch, but by that time I knew something was seriously wrong.

When I entered the cafeteria, which is usually the noisiest room in the school, there was a hushed silence. I just thought the students were waiting to see what would happen next between me and Billy. As far as I was concerned, nothing was going to happen. I had talked the day's events over with Charles the night before, and we had both come to the conclusion that I wouldn't get any more trouble from Billy and that I should leave him alone. He had had his chance to get even with me in the car and instead had acted very nice and just taken me home. It was Charles's considered opinion that a truce was in effect.

What was very strange was that just about every girl was looking at me as though waiting for fireworks to start, but every single boy was totally ignoring me. I could have been invisible as far as they were concerned. I looked over at the football players' table as I passed it, but no one said, "Hey, Tobey," or even looked my way. Billy did glance up at me briefly, but it was with an enigmatic look that left me even more confused.

Katie Lou's table, including herself, was all smiles, which tended to worry me even more than the silence. I sat down with the cheerleaders. Karen made some remark to me, and the cafeteria got back to normal. For a moment there I thought it really had been paranoia on my part. It could be I was getting so used to being the center of attention that I was beginning to construe even silence as relating to me.

"I wonder why everything got so quiet like that," I remarked to the cheerleaders.

"Don't you know, Tobey?"

"Is there something I should know?"

Karen looked at the others and then back at me. "It's that interview you gave. Haven't you seen the paper?"

I shook my head, and she slid a copy of it across the table to me. I scanned it quickly, then looked up in outrage. "He said that was off the record!"

"Oh, that part's just about Billy Rafferty. I don't think anyone cares about that. Actually, it's kind of funny."

"Then what's the fuss all about?"

Karen gave me a rueful smile. "Well, I just don't think you can call half the population stupid and not get some reaction to it."

"Why not? It's the truth!"

"The truth isn't always going to make you popular," said one of the other girls.

"Well, too bad if their egos can't take it." I was really thankful I hadn't said anything derogatory about cheerleaders. That would have left me with only one friend in the entire school.

"I just wouldn't want to be in your shoes during football practice today," said Karen.

I thought about that and decided I didn't want to be either. I was very glad I had said the coaching staff was intelligent, at least. I'd hate for Coach McKeever to pull a silent act on me. However, he could very well construe my interview as not personifying team spirit.

My geometry class, which was about three-fourths boys, also gave me the silent treatment. I took my seat in the back next to Charles, and even he didn't look delighted to see me.

"You really put your foot in your mouth this time, Tobey," he said to me.

"I spoke the truth, Charles, and I'll stand by it."

"Well, I guess your version of the truth and mine just don't happen to coincide."

"What did I say that you don't agree with?"

"I just don't happen to think girls are smarter than boys. In fact I think just the opposite."

"Are you taking it personally, Charles? I said I knew one or two intelligent boys—that meant *you.*"

I guess we were talking kind of loudly, and our teacher, Mr. Allen, asked if we could please settle down in the back.

"I realize I'm just an unintelligent male teacher, but I'd still appreciate your attention, Tobey."

I felt like crawling under my desk and hiding. I hadn't thought the teachers would be stupid enough to take it seriously.

Charles started writing furiously in his notebook. About halfway through the class he handed me this four-page note. On it he had listed all these men's names, starting with Einstein, and asked if I could match those names with the names of equally intelligent women. I hadn't even heard of most of the names, which made me think they were probably scientists.

I did not have the time, the inclination or the knowledge to match up his list, so I simply slid it inside my notebook and ignored it. Maybe that night I could get my mother to supply some names for me.

Gym class turned out to be the only one where I wasn't treated like a leper. The girls, in fact, were overly enthusiastic about my interview. There was talk of starting a girls' football team, and they seemed to think I'd be overjoyed about it. But the truth of the matter was, I'd much rather be the only girl on the boys' team. I think it's that I feel more competitive with boys.

Football practice was almost a total fiasco. I think Coach McKeever would have liked everyone to forget about the interview and just get on with the practice, but that wasn't to be. My first shock came when I saw that Wynn wasn't at practice. Then I remembered he had told me on Monday about a dentist's appointment. As he was my only real friend on the team, I began to feel very isolated.

Ted had always been nice to me, but when the coach asked us to start practicing, Ted said, "I don't know, coach, I think maybe I'm too stupid to hold the ball for Tobey. You know, like I might drop it or something. Maybe you should find some girl to hold it for her—someone with some intelligence."

I could see the other boys were enjoying this immensely.

One of the other boys said, "Maybe you ought to make her quarterback, since Wynn isn't here. After all, she is the only one on the team who isn't stupid, right, coach?"

"No, not quarterback," said one of the others. "She better be one of the receivers. After all, girls run faster than boys—everyone knows that."

Coach McKeever folded his arms over his chest and looked at me. I'm sure he was regretting the day he let me on the team. "I can't say that I was pleased with that interview, Tobey."

"I said the coaching staff was intelligent," I pointed out.

"Yes, I read that. But I also feel a certain loyalty to my own sex. You know which sex I'm talking about—the one without the intelligence."

That got a lot of laughs from the boys.

"I'll tell you, Tobey," the coach continued, "there's no way I can prove to you at the moment that girls aren't smarter than boys, but I think I can prove one thing. I believe you also stated that 'girls are faster,' didn't you?" He waited for my nod before he continued. "Well, I think I can prove you wrong in that right now. And then maybe we can get back to practice."

It turned out that we were going to have a 100-yard race right down the length of the football field. I had one advantage in that I was wearing running shoes and the boys weren't, but I was afraid that wouldn't be enough of an advantage. Ordinarily, I probably would have thought I could beat them all in a race, but after being beaten by Billy the day before, I was no longer so confident.

I happened to know that two of the black guys on the team were also stars of the track team, and one of them held the high school record in the hurdles. For all I knew, the whole team might go out for track. I hadn't really followed the school track team that closely, just what I had read in the papers.

Coach McKeever positioned himself at one end of the field and had his assistant coaches line the team up at the other end. I caught Billy's eye, and he gave me a wink. I knew he was thinking of our race of the previous day. Today, though, I vowed to beat him.

The coach's whistle signaled the start of the race, and I took off down the field as fast as I could go. The football uniform was a hindrance, but I couldn't complain, because we were all wearing it. I was glad I had done so much running during the summer, because by the time I got to the 50-yard line I wasn't even winded. It was a warm day, though, and I sure was sweating.

I never looked behind me at all, because that would have slowed me down, but there were only a couple of guys ahead of me and several neck-to-neck. I just knew most of the guys on the team were carrying too much weight to run that fast. Of course, I had thought the same of Billy, but then he wasn't really heavy, just muscular. Well, I was fairly muscular myself from having lifted Charles's weights for more than six months.

When I got to the 20-yard line I was breathing hard, but I knew I had to make the extra effort. I pretended I was running a personal race against Billy Rafferty, and that was the incentive needed to summon up one last burst of speed that carried me over the finish line. Fourth. The two guys on the track team came in first and second, and Billy, to my annoyance, came in third. Still, I could see by the coach's face that he hadn't expected me to come in anything but last.

All he said to me was, "Maybe you ought to go out for the track team," but that was said with a growl.

The two guys on the track team actually patted me on the back and told me I ran a good race. Billy didn't say anything, but he had a smug smile on his face that I felt like wiping off. The other boys were even less thrilled with me than they had been at the start of the race, particularly when the coach told them they were going to have to do more running during practice and that he was ashamed of them for letting a *girl* beat them. He said "girl" in a way that made me know he was a chauvinist at heart. Nevertheless, that chauvinist had let me on the team, so I wasn't going to complain.

Ted, amidst lots of grumbling, held the ball for me while I practiced my kicks. After that the coach let me play quarterback for a while, as we went over the plays he had devised for me. And then it came time for me to practice my throwing with Billy, and I thought for sure he'd put up a stink. I could see all the other guys watching to see what he'd do.

He didn't do anything, just gave me this evil grin and said, "I guess it's that time, honey."

I wasn't going to use any more of those sarcastic endearments, but I guess he didn't know that.

"I told you you should go out for the track team," he said as he was returning the ball to me.

"Are *you* on it?" I asked him.

"Sure am. So is Wynn."

"What does Wynn go out for?"

"The mile. And he could have beat you today, too."

I didn't mind hearing that; I didn't feel particularly competitive towards Wynn. "What do you go out for?"

"The pole vault."

"No kidding?"

He nodded.

"I bet I could do the pole vault."

"The trouble with you, Tobey, is that you think you can do anything."

"I *can* do anything."

He laughed. "I'll challenge you to the pole vault any day . . . darling."

I found that it was unnerving holding an ordinary conversation with Billy Rafferty. I liked it better when we were fighting and was hoping it would soon get back on that level.

"Knock off the 'darling.' I like it better when you're being your usual nasty self."

"I'm aware of that, sweetheart."

He didn't even seem upset about my interview, and of anyone, he had the most right to be upset. Hadn't I called him the stupidest boy in the whole world?

"How come you're not mad about the interview, Rafferty?"

"I just considered the source. Also, I'm the one who's going to be interviewed next week."

That succeeded in shutting me up. I could just imagine what he was going to say about me. Maybe I'd just be absent from school that day.

After practice, when we went to the gym the coach gave us all a big talk about team spirit and sticking together and "all for one and one for all," and a whole lot of other stuff all directed at me. I figured I deserved it, so I didn't even start an argument. Anyway, it would have been me against everybody, and those aren't the greatest odds.

Since Wynn was absent and I didn't have a ride home, I didn't even go near the parking lot. Instead I went out the front of the school and headed for downtown.

I hadn't gone a block and a half when Billy's car pulled up to the curb, and he asked me if I wanted a ride. He had two guys in the back seat, but none in the front, which made me wonder if he had it all planned out.

"I can get the bus," I told him.

"Hey, you heard the coach—all for one and one for all. Don't you want to ride with your teammates."

His friends were snorting with laughter. It just shows their level of intelligence that they found Billy witty.

I decided not to be churlish about it and got into the car next to Billy. He had the radio on, and they were discussing football. To my relief, the interview was never even mentioned. Billy dropped me off first and just waved away my thanks. The other guys even said, "See you tomorrow," when I left. Then, getting paranoid again, I wondered why they were so nice to me. The awful thought came to me that maybe they had really believed me yesterday when I went off alone with Billy. Or maybe he had told them things about me that weren't true. And maybe I was being paranoid!

At dinner I told everyone about the interview in the school paper, and then I got it and read it to them.

"Is that really true, Tobey?" Robin asked me.

"Of course it is," I told her.

"Girls are smarter than boys?"

"You should be able to tell that even in the fifth grade. Aren't the girls the best readers?"

She nodded.

"And don't they get the best grades?"

She nodded. "Except for Elwood Keefer, but he's weird."

My mother was looking pretty amused, but I noticed that my father wasn't.

"I think I have to take exception to that interview, Tobey. Am I to gather that you think your mother's smarter than I am?"

I looked at my mother and then at my dad. "Well, I guess you two are about equal," I said diplomatically.

This didn't seem to appease him. "And you really believe girls are faster."

"I *proved* that. We had a race and I beat the whole team—except for three boys who are all on the track team."

He looked at my mother. "This is your doing, not mine."

"Don't you think," said my mother, "that you should have thought before you spoke?"

"I *did* think before I spoke. Everything I said is the exact truth."

"Well, Tobey, since they were nice enough to let you on the team, don't you think you owe them something? Like maybe loyalty?"

"No, I don't think so at all. The only reason I made the team was because I'm good. What am I supposed to act like, some token girl who's grateful for the chance? I don't see why I should be treated any differently from the boys. They don't go around acting nice and polite and grateful."

She sighed. "You have a point there, Tobey."

"Wasn't that Billy Rafferty who drove you home today?" asked Robin, the family gossip.

"Yes."

"I thought you hated him."

"I *do* hate him."

"Then how come you let him drive you home?"

"Because Wynn wasn't at practice, and I needed a ride home. How about you?" I asked her, trying to change the subject. "Have you got a boyfriend yet?"

"I have three."

Robin is definitely the femme fatale of the family.

After dinner I showed Mom the list Charles had made out and asked her for her help. She sat down and quickly filled in female names after every man's name, then handed it back to me.

"I never heard of any of them," I told her. "Who are they?"

"They're all professors at Northwestern. But don't worry, Charles won't know that. Just tell him they are all authorities in their fields."

Charles was not impressed. "I never heard of these women—what've they ever done?"

"They are all authorities in their fields," I told him smugly.

"Yeah? What fields?"

"What difference does it make? I didn't ask you about all those men you wrote down."

Charles was still upset with me about the interview. He wasn't overjoyed to hear how well I had done in the race, either.

"I don't know—I'm beginning to think you and Rafferty have a lot in common."

"Thanks a lot, Charles!"

"You're both alike. You're both show-offs, you both have to win all the time and you both have big mouths."

"I'm not a bully."

"You were just as much a bully as he was when you were a kid."

"I think you're being really hateful, Charles."

"How come when I don't say what you want to hear, I'm suddenly being hateful?"

"You used to be nicer to me."

"You used to be nicer, before all this notoriety went to your head."

I decided I'd better be careful. If Charles stopped liking me, I wouldn't have a friend left in the entire school—except Wynn, but maybe he was ticked off about the interview, too.

"Are you sure you don't want to go to Wynn's party?" I asked Charles. I knew very well he didn't want to go, but I wanted to bring the subject around to the party.

"No thanks."

"Why not?"

"Because I'd probably be the only sophomore boy there."

"I'll be there."

"Yes, but you're not a boy, no matter how hard you try to be."

"I do not try to be a boy!"

"Let's not get into another argument, Tobey."

"Do you think Wynn Neil will kiss me at the party?" I tried to say it very casually, as though it were of no importance at all.

"I don't want to talk about it."

"That's what best friends are for, Charles. If I can't talk about it with you, who am I going to talk about it with?"

"That's your problem. I'm just not interested in hearing that kind of talk."

"It's just that it's still new to me, Charles. Once the novelty's worn off, I'm sure I won't want to talk about it."

"When will that be, when you've kissed every boy in the school?"

"I've only kissed you and Wynn."

"So far. And I wish you wouldn't include my kiss."

"Want to try it again?"

"Tobey!"

"Well, I need some more practice before Saturday night."

"Then practice on Billy Rafferty!"

I made a gagging noise and fell to the floor, clutching my stomach. Just the thought of kissing Billy Rafferty made me ill.

After that we lifted weights for a while, and then I went home. My father was out in front washing the car, and I grabbed a sponge and started to help him.

"Do you know what I'd like for Christmas, Dad?"

"It's only September, Tobey."

"Yeah, but do you know what I'd like?"

"I can hardly wait to hear."

"A pole vault."

"A what?"

"I don't know what you call it, but whatever pole vaulters use. What's it called, anyway?"

"Don't ask me, I'm just a stupid man. Your mother, with her vast intelligence, would probably be able to tell you."

"Aren't you ever going to forgive me for that?"

Dad smiled. "You're forgiven. But what's with this pole vaulting?"

I shrugged. "I just thought I might go out for it."

"I've never heard of a woman pole vaulter."

Now that's what I liked to hear. I'd be the very first one, and I would vault ten times higher than Billy Rafferty. I might even break the world record!

Robin stuck her head out the door and said, "Dumb Wynn Neil's on the phone for you."

"Don't call him dumb," I told her.

"I didn't call him dumb; he called himself dumb. He told me to tell you it was dumb Wynn Neil."

So much for Wynn not having seen the article.

"Hey, Tobey, I hear you're going in for the hundred-yard dash these days." He sounded as though he were in a good mood, so I started to relax.

"That was the coach's idea, not mine."

"I wish I had been there. Of course I'm dumb and slow, so . . ."

"Come on, Wynn. I said in the interview that we had intelligent players in the positions that required intelligence. I meant the quarterback, you know."

"You don't have to reassure me, Tobey; I didn't feel threatened. How'd it go with Rafferty yesterday? I was worried about you."

"It went all right. Actually, we're almost getting along these days."

"Too bad—I was hoping your feud would liven up my party."

I was hoping Wynn and I would liven up the party, but of course I didn't say that.

"Is he your boyfriend, Tobey?" Robin asked me when I had hung up.

"Time will tell, Robin," I told her. Just some more words of wisdom to the young.

8

Thursday was an absolutely blah day. Nothing happened at all for the first time in days, and I found the lack of excitement boring. As it turned out, it was the quiet before the storm.

On Friday morning the only thing that happened of any importance was that I passed a Spanish vocabulary test that I was sure I was going to flunk. Some of the kids write the vocabulary words on their arms and then pull their sleeves down, and I was going to try that, but at the last minute I chickened out. I was afraid I might get caught and thrown off the team. But I passed the test anyway, which was a real surprise to me.

You know how on the "Johnny Carson Show" Ed always says, "Here's Johnny," and he always drags out the "here"? Well, when I walked by the

football players' table in the cafeteria that day, all
the boys at the table went, "Here's Tobey!" just the
same way. You know who was sitting right in the
middle of them. A lot of the kids in the cafeteria
applauded when they did that, and even the cheerleaders seemed to think it was cute. But then some
girls think everything is "cute."

The cheerleaders were all going to Wynn's party,
and that's all they talked about that day. They
asked me if I'd ever been to one of Wynn's parties
before, although they must have known I hadn't. I
told them no. Karen said he gave the very best
parties, because there was always lots of food, and
his parents let him serve beer as long as none of the
boys got drunk. At the last party Wynn had, the
lights had been off for forty-five straight minutes.
Karen knew, because her date had timed it.

They didn't have to explain to me what happened when the lights went out; I had a pretty good
idea. I just hoped that when they did go out I'd be
near Wynn Neil. One of the girls also mentioned
that Wynn had a complete collection of *Rolling
Stones* albums, and then they began to talk about
which boys were the best dancers. I am not a good
dancer at all, mainly because I've never gotten any
practice, so I tuned out when they started talking
about that.

I did think that maybe Charles would practice
dancing with me that night, but on second thought,
if he wouldn't practice kissing, he probably
wouldn't practice dancing, either.

I asked them whether they knew if Suzanna was

going to the party, and Karen said she was sure she was. Then she said she thought it very sad that Suzanna and Wynn had broken up, because she thought they were such a perfect couple and so cute together. One of the other girls said she had heard Suzanna's parents had made her break up with Wynn because they were afraid they were getting too serious. When I heard that, I said a silent prayer of thanks to Suzanna's parents.

Anyway, I thought Wynn and I made a cute couple.

In geometry, Charles passed me a note that said in big letters, BE PREPARED!!!!

I wrote back, "What's that supposed to mean?"

Then he wrote back, "It's the Boy Scout motto."

I knew it was the Boy Scout motto; I just didn't know why he was writing it to me. "What are you trying to tell me, Charles," I wrote back.

"Just a warning, that's all."

"What do you know that I don't know."

He gave me a mysterious look. "Just be prepared, Tobey, that's all."

That gave me something to think about the rest of geometry.

I was prepared all through P.E., and nothing happened.

Last period was another pep rally in the auditorium. Even before I got there, I began to get the feeling that I was soon going to find out what I should have prepared for.

There was a murmur when I entered the auditorium. As I headed for the stage, where I was required to sit with the team, the murmur grew louder and louder. Then, when I started up the steps to the stage, I saw what the murmuring was all about.

Every single member of the team—even Wynn —was wearing an orange t-shirt that said in large, blue letters: TOBEY TYLER DOES IT ALL.

I looked over and saw that Coach McKeever and his assistants were also wearing them. I turned around and started to head back down the steps, planning on spending the assembly time hiding out in the girls' washroom.

Coach McKeever's voice stopped me. "Come on back here, Tobey," he said.

Then the whole team, in perfect unison, chanted, "Come on back here, Tobey."

Then the whole school—well, you get the idea.

If I had been asleep, this would have rated as a nightmare.

I went back and took my place in the front row, hoping my face wasn't as red as it felt. I swear I'll get you for this, Billy Rafferty, I vowed to myself. I had only embarrassed him in front of his friends; he had embarrassed me in front of the entire school!

My eyes traveled over the audience until I spotted Charles sitting near the back. He was laughing along with everybody else, the traitor. I know boys stick together, but I had thought Charles was different. He could have done more than just tell me to be prepared. How can you prepare if you don't know what to prepare against? If he had told me, I would have cut the assembly and gladly taken the consequences.

It's hard to believe, but the worst was yet to come.

The principal made his little speech (he, at least, wasn't wearing one of the t-shirts), we sang the Evanston fight song and then the assembly was turned over to Coach McKeever. He almost immediately turned the assembly over to me, saying, "I think Tobey would like to say a few words to you about the game tomorrow."

Forget Billy Rafferty! At that moment it was the coach I wanted to kill. If there's anything I absolutely hate, it's getting up in front of people and having to talk. The whole audience was applauding this announcement, though, so I knew I was going to have to brazen it out.

I got up out of my chair and walked over to the microphone, which was too tall for me, but I didn't care if I was heard anyway. They wanted a few words? I'd give them a few words.

"We're going to win tomorrow," I said, and while they were cheering that bit of news, I started to walk back to my seat. But then there were cries of "More! More!"

I turned around and looked out at the audience. "You want more?" I shouted.

"Yes!" they shouted back as one.

Being a natural show-off, I was starting to get into this.

I went back to the microphone. "Do you want to know why we're going to win?" I asked them.

"Tell us, Tobey," someone yelled out.

"Because we have a coach who's probably the best coach in the entire state!" I waited until the cheering died down, and then added, "Even if he is something of a male chauvinist!"

There was lots of cheering from the girls at that and a lot of laughing from the boys. And I have to admit I was beginning to eat it up.

"You want to know why else we're going to win?"

"Tell us, Tobey!"

I turned around and looked in Wynn's direction. "Because we have a fairly intelligent quarterback," I told them. "For a boy!"

Wynn gave me a wry smile before getting up to take a bow.

"And now I have another surprise for you," I told the audience, and there was some more applause. "Everybody's darling, Evanston High's answer to Joe Namath, yes, Billy Rafferty himself, is now going to come over to the microphone and explain to you tomorrow's game plan. Let's hear it for Billy Rafferty!"

I led in the applause as I turned to Billy and waited for him to turn as red as I was when he found his strategy had backfired on him.

Billy didn't look embarrassed at all, which just goes to prove he's more of a show-off than I am. He got out of his seat, smiled at me and inclined his head to the applause, then came over and stood beside me. I started to move away, thinking I had done my part, but he put his arm around my shoulders and wouldn't let me move.

He began to speak, and he sounded very sure of himself. "First of all, let me say how pleased I am that Tobey would admit a boy had enough intelligence to even try to explain our game plan to you."

The audience roared with laughter.

"Well, I'll tell you what the thrust of our game plan is, and that's this cute little girl standing next to me. Little Tobey Tyler is going to be our secret weapon!"

Cute? Little? I was going to kill him!

The audience loved it.

"I'll tell you the truth. I wasn't too pleased at first about having a girl on the team. But now? Well, I just don't know how we ever got along without her. As my t-shirt says, Tobey Tyler does it all!"

"Aren't you laying it on a little thick," I hissed at him. The microphone picked it up, and everyone laughed. I bit my lip in frustration.

"Now I know you haven't believed a word I've said. And I know for sure Tobey hasn't believed a word I've said, but what I'm going to say now is the truth, I swear. Football practice has never been as much fun as it's been this year."

There was more laughter and applause at that, and while it was dying down, Billy motioned for the other guys to come down and join us. I didn't know what was happening until we were all lined up on the stage, with me and Billy in the middle, and they all started doing my cheer. The real one, thank heavens, not Billy's version.

I didn't blame the audience for laughing, as the boys were all kicking their legs up in the air and imitating the cheerleaders while they did it. I just stood there, not wanting to cheer for myself.

Then the assembly was dismissed. As we walked out, I said to Billy, "Where's my t-shirt?"

"Don't worry, I've got one for you."

"I suppose you're the one who had them made up?"

"Did you have any doubt?"

"No."

"I thought you'd be mad at me over this."

I looked up at him in surprise. "You think I'm not?"

"You're not acting very mad."

"Ah, but beneath this calm exterior, my mind is thinking of only one thing."

"What's that?"

"How to get even with you."

"Good. I was afraid for a moment there you were mellowing."

"Listen, Billy, would you do me a favor?"

"You're asking me for a favor?"

I didn't even realize where we were until I suddenly noticed I was about to walk into the boys' locker room. I stopped and backed off a few feet. "I'm serious, Billy. This is totally apart from our feud and wishing you dead when I was up on that stage."

"Let's hear it."

"Do you have the stuff at home for pole vaulting?"

"Sure."

"Could I try it?"

"I can't let you do that."

I felt an unreasonable anger flare up in me. "You're selfish, Billy Rafferty."

He gave a groan. "And you're the most unreasonable person I know. The easiest way to sprain an ankle is to try pole vaulting when you don't know what you're doing. The coach would have my neck if I was responsible for your being hurt."

"You're just afraid I might be able to do it."

"Tobey, I'm not even allowed to do it during football season."

"Thanks a lot, Billy Rafferty. I ask you one little favor in my whole entire life, and you turn me down. Thanks a lot—I really mean it." I turned and ran down the hall before he could say something else reasonable. I just didn't feel like hearing reasonable excuses from Billy Rafferty.

The team was friendlier to me at practice that day than they'd ever been. I think for two reasons, really. First they had effectively gotten back at me for my interview by staging that little performance in the auditorium. And second, I had taken it like a good sport and hadn't broken down and cried, which would have been acting the way they expected a girl to act. So now, for the first time, they were all treating me like a buddy. I don't know how Billy was treating me, because I was ignoring Billy.

I did my kicking practice with Ted, I did my short stint at being quarterback in case the coach decided to use that play, and then once again Billy and I were sent off for me to practice passing.

"Good throw," Billy yelled to me when he caught my first pass.

I ignored him.

The second pass he caught in a leaping play that I should have congratulated but didn't.

After that I threw and he caught in silence for about twenty minutes. Then it seemed like Billy couldn't take it any longer.

"All right, you win," he yelled at me.

"What do I win?"

"Come on over tonight, and you can try the pole vault. What do I care if you break your neck?"

I tried not to look smug. "Thank you, Billy, that's very nice of you to ask me."

"Don't come on with that 'sweet' act of yours with me, Tyler."

That made me laugh out loud, and my last pass of the day was way off the mark.

Wynn drove me home after practice. I was busting to tell him what I was going to do that night, but then I thought better of it. He'd probably just tell me I was crazy to risk injury.

I ate dinner as fast as I could that night. When I got up to leave the table, my mother said, "Are you going over to see Charles?"

I had forgotten all about Charles! "Later," I told

her, hoping Charles wouldn't get mad when I showed up later than usual. All we were planning to do was watch television.

I must have felt guilty about it, though, because I went out the back way and down the alley until I got to Billy's house. He was already in the back-yard, and he was placing this pole over two other poles, and it looked awfully high up in the air to me. Behind the poles were some mats that I guess he fell on.

"Hi, Billy," I said.

He turned around. "I figured you'd show up."

"Were you hoping I wouldn't?"

"As a matter of fact, I was. I still think this is pretty stupid."

"Well, you think everything I do is stupid anyway."

"You may have a point."

I do think everything he does is stupid, so we were even.

I had changed into jeans and a sweatshirt, and he was dressed the same. I sat down in the grass and waited for him to demonstrate for me.

He picked up a very long pole and walked over to where I was sitting. "I want you to watch me very carefully while I do this, Tobey. I want you to watch how I run and at what point I start to vault and the position my body is in when I go over the pole. Most importantly, I want you to watch how I fall, because if you fall the wrong way, you can really hurt yourself."

"Okay."

He sighed. "How about the hurdles or the high jump? Wouldn't you rather try them?"

"No. I want to learn how to pole vault."

"I suppose it's no use telling you I don't know of any girls who do this."

I just smiled.

"All right, Tobey—it's your neck." He went a long way back in his yard, then he started off with a run, the pole in his hands. I tried to watch everything he told me, but it all went so fast I couldn't. One minute he was putting the end of the pole on the ground, and the next his body was flying way up in the air and clearing the pole. He went up so high and it was so graceful I found myself holding my breath. When he fell, he landed on his back. I ran over to see if he was all right.

"Are you okay, Billy?" I asked, kneeling down beside him.

His blue eyes were gleaming. "Yeah, I'm okay." He pushed himself up on his elbows. "Did you see how I did it?"

"It was awfully fast. Could you show me a little slower?"

He collapsed back on the mat. "I don't believe you!"

"All right, never mind. Just let me have the pole, and I'll give it a try."

I started to reach out for the pole, and he grabbed me by my wrist. "Let's talk about this, Tobey."

"There's nothing to talk about. You told me I could do it."

"Would you just answer me one question first?"

"What?"

"Why do you want to do it?"

"Why not?"

"I want an answer, not another question. Go on, think about it, but I want to know what reason you have for wanting to try to pole vault."

"Let go of my wrist. I'm not going to run away with your pole."

He dropped my wrist, and our eyes locked while I tried to think of a reason that would satisfy him.

"Do you want me to tell you the reason?"

I gave him a suspicious look. What was he up to now?

"Do you want me to, Tobey?"

I shrugged.

"For as long as I've known you, you've always tried to beat me at everything. You just can't stand it when I can do something you can't do."

"That's when we were little kids, Billy. Give me a break!"

"Then what do you call this?"

"It just sounded like fun, that's all."

"What are you trying to do, be like me?"

"Are you crazy?"

"Just think about it, okay?"

He got up and handed me the pole. "I'm going to lower the pole and start you off at five feet."

"That's for babies!"

"No, it's for beginners." He went over and spent some time adjusting the pole, then showed me how to grip the pole.

"Remember to flip your body when you go over, Tobey, and try to relax when you fall. If you're relaxed, the chances of your hurting yourself are much less."

I don't even know how to describe my first attempt. I hit the pole straight on, sending it flying and me sprawling on my face on the mat. When I raised myself up and looked over at Billy, I could tell he was trying not to laugh.

"All right, so I did something wrong."

"You did just about everything wrong. I'll do it again, and you pay attention this time." He put the pole back up and backed up from it a few yards. "Just watch the way my body goes over, okay?"

First of all, his body was straight when he went over, but I didn't really see how he managed that. I guessed I'd just have to concentrate on telling my body to straighten out.

After about an hour and more attempts than I care to describe, I finally made it over the pole without knocking it down.

"I did it, Billy, I did it!" I yelled, running over to him.

He reached out and mussed up my hair. "You always were the bravest little kid in the neighborhood."

"Raise it higher!"

"What?"

"Raise it some more. I want to break my record."

He gave me a look of incredulity. "Tobey, it took you thirty-six tries to even make it."

"Just a couple of inches, okay?"

He looked at his watch. "I really can't, Tobey; I'm supposed to be somewhere. In fact, I'm late now."

I could feel my lower lip begin to stick out. "Oh, sorry. I guess you have a date with one of those blondes you like to play with, right?"

"Not tonight, no. It's just that the guys usually get together for a while the night before a game. Listen, you're on the team—you want to come along?"

I shook my head. "No, I'm supposed to go over and see Charles."

"Okay, see you tomorrow then. And listen, Tobey, if you want a ride to the game tomorrow, just come by my house about noon. Okay?"

"Yeah. Thanks, Billy. I will."

I ran all the way to Charles's house. It was dark already, and I figured he'd be really mad at me. Particularly since I hadn't had much time for him lately.

He didn't seem mad, and so I told him about the pole vaulting.

"*Billy* taught you how?"

"Yeah, honest."

"Are you two friends now?"

"No, I still hate him. But he was pretty nice to me tonight."

"Probably because you were pretty nice to him for a change."

"Oh, come on, Charles. I'm not the one who starts everything."

"You want to lift some weights?"

"I don't know; I'm pretty tired. You do it and I'll just rest up for the game." I sprawled out on his lower bunk bed while he started pumping iron. That's a silly name for it, I think, but that's what his book calls it.

I can't talk while I lift weights, because I have to concentrate on my breathing, but Charles can do both at the same time. So now he said, "I have a date tomorrow night."

"Oh, sure."

"I just thought I'd let you know, that's all."

"Are you serious, Charles?"

"I'm always serious."

Yeah, that's true, he is. "Who with?"

"Her name is Nancy Kimmons. She's a freshman."

"Are you serious, Charles?"

"All right, forget it. I just thought that since you're my best friend, I'd tell you, that's all."

"Where did you meet Nancy Kimmons?"

"In Science Club."

"You don't belong to Science Club."

"I do now."

"How come I haven't heard any of this?"

"If you'll recall, Tobey, all we've been talking about lately is you. You're the celebrity in the crowd."

In other words, he was pointing out to me that I was self-centered. "So why did you join Science Club?"

"Why not? Once you started football practice, I didn't have anything to do after school."

"You could have gone out for some sport."

"I don't like sports. I like science."

"And you're really going out with some girl?"

"I said I was."

"How'd you ask her?"

"What do you mean, how'd I ask her?"

"What did you say?"

"We were both talking about wanting to see this science fiction movie that's playing, and I asked her if she wanted to go with me."

"*I* wanted to see that movie."

"Maybe you can get Wynn to take you to it."

Touché, Charles! Keep it up, and I'll walk right out of here. I didn't see why all of a sudden Charles had to start dating just because I was interested in Wynn Neil. I hadn't even had a real date yet, and girls are supposed to start dating earlier than boys.

"Is your father going to drive you?"

"She doesn't mind going on the bus."

She was beginning to sound very dumb to me. "Is she pretty?"

"I don't know."

"Haven't you even looked at her?"

"I don't know, Tobey—I like her, that's all."

"I thought boys liked girls who were pretty."

"Maybe some do; I don't. I like a girl I can talk

154

to, and Nancy's very easy to talk to. She's kind of like you, only she likes science."

"Are we still going to be best friends?"

"Of course we are. You just don't have much time for me anymore, and I was getting bored."

"Football season won't last forever."

"Oh sure, and after that you'll probably go out for pole vaulting."

He was right, I probably would.

"Are you going to the game tomorrow?"

"Of course I am. You don't think I'd miss that, do you?"

I guess I didn't know what to think anymore. Somehow I had never thought Charles would start dating. I thought he'd always be there for me.

"Are you going to kiss her?"

"That's none of your business, Tobey, and if you're thinking of getting in some more practice, you can just forget it. Practice on Wynn."

When I got home, Robin said, "I saw you go down to Billy's tonight."

"So what?"

"I think you have three boyfriends, just like me: Wynn and Charles and Billy."

At the moment I would have settled for just one.

9

I woke up early Saturday morning feeling stiff. At first I thought it was due to the fact that Grogan had spent the night sleeping alternately on my back and on my legs, but I found out in the shower that I had several bruises on my body. It must have been from the pole vaulting or, to be more accurate, the pole vaulting attempts, but I didn't mind. I figured a few bruises befit a football player, even if I hadn't gotten them in the line of duty, so to speak.

I stood under the hot shower a long time, then turned on the cold for the few minutes that I could stand it. The stiffness was gone by the time I got out. By eight o'clock I was dressed in my football uniform and down in the kitchen. Everyone else was still asleep, but I had been too excited. The thought of not only a football game but also

Wynn's party had me in a charged-up state of excitement.

I opened a can of nasty-smelling tuna for Grogan and filled his water dish, then got the box of Frosted Flakes out of the cupboard. I poured a huge bowlful, then sliced a banana on top. A little additional sugar, some milk and I was all set.

As I ate, I fantasized myself doing a Frosted Flakes commercial dressed in my football uniform. I thought briefly of writing the manufacturers of Frosted Flakes a letter offering my services, but then remembered how I hate to write letters. Well, maybe they'd hear of me on their own.

After breakfast I rinsed out my bowl, then went upstairs and made my bed. I don't really think football stars should have to make their own beds, but try telling that to my mother.

It was still only eight-thirty, and I couldn't think of anything to do until it was time to leave at noon. I thought of going across the street and waking Charles up, but that would mean also waking his parents, and they're real grouches in the morning. For that matter, Charles is a real grouch in the morning.

I let myself out the back door and into the yard. The sun was out, and it was going to be perfect weather for football. I went out the back gate and headed across the field to the alley. I thought I'd just maybe walk by Billy's house in case he was out in back practicing the pole vault. Not that I thought he really would be.

I was standing looking over his back fence when

I saw his kitchen window being opened. I was really embarrassed to be seen there by his mother or his sisters, so I crouched down behind some bushes.

A minute later the back door opened and Billy came out on the stoop. He was wearing only pajama bottoms. "What are you doing, Tobey, spying on me?"

I straightened up, keeping my eyes on his face and not on his pajama bottoms. "I thought maybe you'd let me practice with your pole vaulting stuff."

"Come on inside and have some coffee."

Coffee? Billy Rafferty drank coffee? That sounded so sophisticated. I was still forced to drink milk at home.

"Come on—I'm freezing standing out here."

I went through the gate, across the yard, up the steps and into the kitchen. It was different from ours. Instead of a built-in breakfast nook, he was sitting at a round table in front of the window.

"Where are your parents?" I asked him.

"Sleeping."

I wondered what they'd think if they came down and found me sitting there with Billy wearing only his pajama bottoms. I knew what my parents would think.

He brought over a cup for me and the coffeepot. "How do you want it?" he asked.

"Black." I thought that sounded more adult than asking for lots of sugar and milk.

He sat down across from me. "What are you doing up so early? You nervous about the game?"

"No, are you?"

"I always get up early."

"I just thought I could practice some more pole vaulting."

"Not until after football season."

"Why not?"

"Because I say so."

Well, if I got my own equipment for Christmas, I wouldn't have to use his. I took a sip of the coffee and burned my tongue.

"What's the matter, you nervous about the game?"

"I think I'm more nervous about Wynn's party than the game," I found myself answering truthfully.

"Why would you be nervous about his party?"

"Well, I've played in one football game already, but I've never been to a high school party."

"I keep forgetting you're just a sophomore."

"What do you do at parties?"

"Look, it'll probably be a victory celebration. All you'll have to do is listen to everyone tell you how great you were."

"What if I'm not great?"

"Then you'll have to listen to everyone tell you how lousy you were. You'll be fine, though, Tobey. You don't have anything to worry about."

I tried the coffee again. It had a nasty taste, and I couldn't understand why people drank so much of it. I'd much rather have a Coke for breakfast, if I had a choice.

"What else will we do there?"

He leaned back in his chair and put his hands behind his neck. The hair under his arms was as red as the hair on his head. "Let me see, what will you do? Well, you'll eat and you'll drink—"

"I don't drink!"

"There'll be plenty of soft drinks there. And there'll be music playing, and someone will ask you to dance. Probably Wynn. And then someone will put the lights out . . ."

"And then what happens?"

He grinned. "Whatever you want, I guess."

I averted my eyes from his and looked out the window. "I'd rather talk about the game."

"Quit worrying about the party, Tobey. The whole team'll be there—you'll be fine. Your friends the cheerleaders will be there, too."

"Karen said you asked her out once."

"Yeah, I had quite a crush on her last year, but she wouldn't go out with me."

"She said it was because you were too young."

"I got over it. Anyway, other than her looks, I find her pretty boring."

"How about Katie Lou Slight? Have you ever asked *her* out?"

"That barracuda?"

I laughed. "Yeah, she scares me, too."

"I don't believe it. You're not scared of anything."

Hearing he thought that of me, I didn't want to disabuse him of the notion. "So who do you have a crush on now?"

"I don't get crushes anymore. I'm too old."

I gave him a disbelieving look.

"I know who you have a crush on, though."

I guess everyone knew. "He's been really nice to me."

"Wynn's a nice guy."

For some reason, I was finding him just as easy to talk to as Charles. In fact, Charles wouldn't have even held this kind of conversation for long.

"Actually, I think he's too nice for you." His evil grin was in effect.

"Thanks a lot, Billy!"

"Just thought I'd throw that in. It was making me nervous getting along so well with you."

I pushed my coffee cup away. "I guess I better get home."

"How about some eggs?"

"Who's going to cook them?"

"Listen, if girls can play football, boys should be able to cook."

I gave him my own evil grin. "Why not? It's a natural progression from playing with dolls, I suppose."

He just laughed and went over to the refrigerator and took out some bacon and eggs. Then he handed me some bread and told me to make the toast. I refuse to do such domestic things at home, but since he could cook, I didn't figure it would kill me to make some toast. I also didn't tell him I'd already eaten breakfast. I couldn't eat right before the game anyway, and it would be a long time until dinner.

He broke the egg yolks and I kind of burned the

toast, but the bacon was perfect, and he even gave me a Coke and threw my coffee down the sink.

Afterwards he said, "Look, Tobey, you want to drive around with me until time for the game?"

"What would you have done if I hadn't come over?"

"Fooled around, maybe read a little."

"You read books?"

"Sure, don't you?"

"Not if I can help it."

"Then you read the wrong kind of books. I'll loan you some you'll like, if you want."

"Okay—not about the books, but about driving around. I'll go tell my parents where I'll be and meet you out in front."

"And listen, Tobey—"

"Yeah?"

"Do you want a ride to the party tonight?"

I hesitated, not knowing what to say.

"Don't worry, I'll make sure everyone knows we're not together, that it's just a ride."

"Okay," I agreed. I just wouldn't have wanted Wynn to think I was fickle.

My dad was up and I told him where I'd be. He said they'd see me after the game. Then I went back to Billy's house and he was already dressed and waiting out in front.

"Just one thing, Tobey."

"What's that?"

"Take your helmet off while we're driving around, will you?"

* * *

I got to kick two field goals and five extra points and we beat New Trier 41–14, but the game was more exciting than it sounds from the score.

First of all, even though a whole lot of people were cheering me because of my being the only girl on the team, I was *not* the star of the game. Wynn threw three touchdown passes and ran himself for another, and he would easily have been voted Most Valuable Player, if we had such a thing. I didn't care that I wasn't the star, because I was getting so much attention I don't think I could have taken any more.

First of all, when I made the very first kickoff of the game, all the guys in the New Trier stands started to whistle at me. Not to be outdone by all that whistling, our cheerleaders got out there and started my cheer. Pretty soon all I heard were whistles and my name being yelled, and for a show-off that's pretty exhilarating stuff, let me tell you. I made a really good kick, and then there wasn't much to do, as our team didn't get the ball for a while.

Then we did get the ball and I kicked the extra point, and the next time we got the ball, I got my first chance to kick a field goal. It wasn't a spectacular one, but it was the first one anyone had seen me kick, so the stands kind of went wild. My mother told me later that Dad got tears in his eyes when I kicked it, but I think it more likely that a piece of dirt blew in his eyes. Dad is not the sentimental type.

The first time we had to punt, I was hoping the

coach would let me pass, but he said no, that we should wait because the New Trier coach was no dummy (despite the fact he was a man) and he'd probably be expecting it.

But the next time it came to a punt, the coach told me to do what we'd been practicing all week—and under *no* circumstances to run with the ball, because he didn't want to see me hurt. I looked over at Billy, and I could see he was thinking the same thing I was thinking; that if the coach knew I'd been jumping over poles, he'd probably have a heart attack.

Well, our coach misjudged New Trier's coach, because they were expecting it all right. No sooner had I dropped back with the ball than three of their players sacked me. They had to get up first, naturally, because I was on the bottom. I waited for them to get up, and then I saw one of them hold out his hand to help me. I thought that was so sporting of him that I let him pull me up. He kept holding on to my hand, though, for no reason, so I finally took a good look at his face. He was one of the cute guys Wynn had introduced me to at the drive-in.

"Oh, hi," I said to him.

"Nice seeing you again, Tobey. Sorry about the tackle."

"That's okay. You were just doing your job." He had a really nice smile, and I think he looked even better in his football uniform than he had in his regular clothes.

"What are you doing tonight?" he asked me.

I couldn't believe this was happening. "Why?"

"We're having a school dance, and we were wondering if you'd want to come. Sort of as our guest of honor."

I thought that was really nice of him, and I was about to tell him so when I noticed our defense was all on the field and we were holding things up. Then Billy came over and said, "You're supposed to play them, Tobey, not date them," and I began to feel a little foolish. Then one of the referees stopped by. I think he wanted to penalize someone for delay of the game, but since he didn't know which team was doing the delaying, he just ordered us off the field.

When I got back to the sidelines, Wynn said, "They're going to have to think up a new penalty for socializing on the field."

"That was one of the guys you introduced me to, remember?"

"It's all right to talk to him at drive-ins, but not during the game."

"Sorry."

"Don't worry about it. This is something that's never come up at our games before. They haven't ever tried to date any of us."

The coach came over and asked me what I had been doing out there. When I told him, he said, "Next time tell them you'll go to the dance if they'll agree not to sack you. I can see we could devise some interesting strategy around your dating habits."

Maybe it was all a joke to him, but it was the first

time a boy had ever actually asked me out. Except maybe he meant the whole team was inviting me. I was sorry now I hadn't asked.

The next time we were in a punt situation, I think they were expecting something again, but this time I got good protection from my own team, and they couldn't get through in time to sack me. I saw Artie Ford in the clear and passed to him, and it was an easy first down. Wynn went on to make a touchdown pass on the very next play, and I could tell he was really pleased with me. I secretly wished I had been the one to make the touchdown pass, but you can't have everything.

The thing about the games I like the least is half time. When I used to be a spectator, I always used that time to get two hot dogs and a Coke, but now I wasn't allowed to eat. Other than going in the school to use the bathroom, I had nothing to do but just sit around and wait for the intermission to be over. New Trier's team came back out on the field before our team. When I saw some of their guys motioning for me to come over, I crossed the field and went over to talk to them.

Their coach was really young and nice, and he asked me if my parents would consider moving so that I could go to school at New Trier. I told him I didn't think so. Then he said that if I would, he'd let me play quarterback once in a while. I told him that was an offer I couldn't refuse and that I'd ask my parents, but I knew very well they'd say no. Anyway, I didn't want to go to New Trier. Everyone at Evanston really hates New Trier.

Then their cheerleaders came over and wanted to meet me. I was standing around talking to them when Coach McKeever showed up and asked me if I was defecting.

I wasn't sure what that meant, so I didn't say anything. Then New Trier's coach said, "I'm giving you fair warning, Mac. I'm going to try to steal her away from you."

Coach McKeever gave me a look like he was beginning to think he wouldn't mind, then he told me to go back where I belonged. I waved good-bye to everyone, then once more crossed the field.

"You're not safe to take out in public," Billy said to me.

"What's the matter with talking to them? They're really nice. They said I could be quarter-back on their team."

"They were just kidding you, Tobey."

"No they weren't, Billy Rafferty! The coach said so himself."

"Be realistic, Tobey. You're too small."

"I'll bet there've been other small quarterbacks in history."

"Name one."

I was glad the game started then, because I couldn't think of one.

It was a very good game all in all, and the funny part was the New Trier kids were cheering me as much as they were cheering their own team. But I guessed they were used to losing and took it better than we did. The following week, though, we would be playing Highland Park, and they were a lot tougher team.

I got a surprise after the game. My grandparents on my mother's side had driven up from Chicago just to see me play, and they took us all out to dinner afterwards. Every time we go out to dinner with them, I'm forced to wear a dress, or at least a skirt, but this time they couldn't say anything, because the only clothes I had with me was my uniform.

My grandfather played football for Michigan State years and years ago, and I could tell he was really proud of me. My grandmother simply thought it was shocking. That's what she kept saying to my mother: "It's simply shocking! The child's going to get killed. I don't understand why you allow her to do it. It's simply shocking."

My mother always just agrees with her and then lets me do what I want. To give you an idea of my grandmother, I always told her I wanted a football for Christmas and she always gave me a doll. My mother used to put them in boxes after Christmas and store them in the linen closet. Luckily, Robin turned out to like dolls, so she ended up with quite a collection.

Even though we went to a nice restaurant, I was allowed to have two hamburgers and two orders of fries for dinner and even a chocolate milk shake. At least we didn't have to stay with them at the restaurant too long, because I had to go home and get ready for the party.

I didn't see Charles, because my parents said he

got a ride home with someone else after the game. I guess he had to go home to get ready for his date.

When I got home, I took a shower and washed my hair and then dressed in my best jeans and my navy blue cashmere sweater with the V neck. Instead of running shoes, I wore my new boots, with the jeans tucked in.

I was ready a half hour too early and got so fidgety I finally walked down to Billy's house.

10

I rang his doorbell, and he answered the door. "Couldn't you wait?" he asked me.

"No."

"Well, come on in. I'm ready, too."

Then, when I came in, he said, "Who changes clothes, you or me?"

"I already changed my clothes, Billy."

"Yeah, but it's going to look kind of strange if we walk in there dressed like twins."

And then I noticed that he was wearing jeans and a navy blue V-neck sweater, just like me. Only he wasn't wearing boots.

"We all wear the same uniforms. What's the difference if we dress the same?"

Then I heard Billy's father calling me from the

living room, so I went in to say hello to him. He said he'd seen the game and was very impressed with my playing. I didn't mind hearing that and was ready to sit down and recap the game with him, but Billy said we might as well leave, so we did.

We picked up two of Billy's friends on the way, and if they were surprised to see me riding in Billy's car, they didn't mention it. I guess they were prepared for almost anything when it came to Billy and me. We talked about the game, of course— that's just the kind of talk I like the best and also the kind I never get from Charles or my family.

Wynn turned out to live farther from my house than I had thought. I definitely didn't live on his way home, as he had led me to believe. It was a nice realization to know he really wanted to take me home, that it wasn't just a convenience for him.

His house was really big, with a lot more land around it than we had. Billy said there were tennis courts in the back, but I didn't get to see them, because we were herded right down in the basement along with some other kids when we arrived.

The basement wasn't bad either. One end had a lot of furniture, just like a living room, and the other end had an enormous stereo system and plenty of room for dancing. In between were two long picnic tables piled with all kinds of food and just about every soft drink you could think of. There were even three kinds of beer in a big styrofoam cooler on the floor.

As soon as I got down in the basement, Wynn

171

came over to me and said he was glad I could make it. As if anything but death would have kept me from his party!

"You want a beer?" he asked me.

"Aren't we supposed to be in training?"

He just laughed and opened a can of Coke and handed it to me. He asked if I would mind helping him pick out some records and putting them on the stereo and said that he wanted to dance with me as soon as he wasn't so busy greeting people.

I hoped he meant a slow dance and not disco. I've just never learned how to do that, but I figure anyone can do a slow dance. Anyway, I wanted to see what it would be like to have his arms around me.

Eddie, one of the guys on the football team who beat me in the race, helped me pick out records, because he seemed to know them better than I did. Then, when this fast music started playing, he asked me if I wanted to dance.

Some other kids had already started to dance, and he told me it was easy. All I had to do was follow him. Well, I tried, but he was probably the best dancer at the party, and there was no way I could keep up with him. After a while, he didn't even seem to notice whether I was still there or not, so I picked up my Coke and went over and sat down on one of the couches.

Two of the cheerleaders were sitting over there, too, and they asked me why I had stopped dancing.

"I'm not very good at it," I told them, which was the understatement of the year.

"Just because you drove me here—"

"If you don't watch it, I'm going to drive you right home!"

Then I noticed everyone was watching us and the dancing had stopped. I guess they were all waiting for me to do something like pour a can of beer over Billy's head. I began to think that might not be a bad idea when Wynn came over and asked me to dance.

Miraculously, it was a slow song, and I felt as though I were floating when Wynn took my hand and pulled me out on the dance floor. He put both arms around my waist, and I put mine around his neck; he kind of rested his chin on top of my head, while my nose stuck into his wool sweater and started to itch.

"I thought you two had quit fighting."

"Oh, Billy and I will never quit fighting. Everything I do annoys him, and everything he does annoys me."

"He drove you here, didn't he?"

"Yeah, but he's probably sorry now. I can always get a ride home with someone else." I was beginning to wish Wynn would stop talking so I could concentrate on how it felt to be in his arms.

"It was a fantastic game today, wasn't it?"

"You were great—all those touchdown passes."

"And your field goal."

I didn't even want to talk football with him. I moved my head so that the wool would quit rubbing against my nose and looked over at the

175

side of the room. I saw Suzanna with some of her friends. She was watching us, looking kind of sad. That made me feel bad, because I didn't want to be the one to make her sad. On the other hand, maybe the reason she looked sad was because her new Northwestern boyfriend wasn't with her, but I really didn't think so. I really think she still liked Wynn. I turned my head the other way so that I didn't have to watch her watching us.

Wynn pulled me closer to him, and I was glad I had moved my head or otherwise my nose would have gotten squashed. And then I began to ask myself why was I thinking about my nose at a time like this. This was one of my fantasies coming true, and I didn't even seem to be enjoying it. I was dancing with the most popular boy in the school and the quarterback of our football team, and it didn't seem any different from dancing with my father at family gatherings—except I couldn't remember my nose ever itching when I danced with my father.

The slow song came to an end. We paused, and then another slow song started right up. I was about to tell Wynn I wanted another beer when Billy tapped him on the shoulder and told him Suzanna wanted to talk to him.

Wynn said, "Excuse me, Tobey, I'll see you later," and went off, and before I could escape, Billy put his arms around me and I was suddenly dancing with him.

"That was a lie, Billy Rafferty. Suzanna's over there talking to her friends."

"Maybe so, but he should be talking to her. People who love each other shouldn't break up for no reason."

"What are you now, Cupid?" Up until this point he had his arms around me, but mine were just hanging at my sides. He moved his and took hold of my wrists, then put them around his neck. Then he put his arms back around me again and held me very close. His sweater wasn't so itchy, though, so my nose was okay. He was bigger than Wynn and more muscular, and for some reason it seemed a lot more exciting to be in his arms than in Wynn's. But I think that was because I was in the arms of the enemy, and that seemed more dangerous. I like danger.

"How come you're dancing so nicely with me, Tobey? I figured you'd yell at me for breaking it up between you and Wynn."

"It's probably because I've been drinking beer and I don't know what I'm doing."

"What you're doing is dancing too close."

"I danced this close with Wynn, and *he* didn't complain!"

"Did you enjoy it?"

Why do boys have to talk so much when they dance?

"It was all right."

"And what about with me? Are you enjoying it?" He pulled back from me and looked down at my face, and I could feel myself flushing. It seemed to be getting very warm in the room.

"I'm just trying to learn how to dance, that's all!"

He gave me his evil smile. "You call this dancing? All we're doing is standing with our arms around each other and swaying a little to the music."

"Are you trying to make me mad, Billy Rafferty? Because if that's what you're trying to do, you're succeeding."

"I don't see you walking away from me."

"I'm thinking about it."

"But you're not doing it."

"Is that a dare?"

He chuckled and pulled me in closer to him again. And I did start to think about walking away from him, but then I felt his lips on top of my head and his warm breath, and I admitted to myself that I didn't really feel like walking away. I was actually quite happy right where I was, not that I would have told Billy Rafferty that!

"You never refuse a dare, do you, Tobey?" His voice sounded low and different somehow. Not quite as annoying as usual.

"Never!"

"And what if I dared you to kiss me?"

I swallowed hard. "You wouldn't dare," I said in a small voice.

"Is that what you think?"

And then some fool turned out the lights, and the basement was plunged into total darkness. "Why'd they do that?" I complained to Billy.

"Why do you think?"

Probably as soon as the lights went out everybody started kissing up a storm. Well, that wasn't for me. I wanted to see what was happening when I got kissed. In the dark it could be just anyone kissing you, and you wouldn't even know the difference.

Billy stopped moving to the music, and we were just standing there. "Well, Tobey?"

"Well what?"

"What are you thinking?"

"I'm thinking I'd like to get out of here. I don't like it in the dark."

"Don't tell me Tobey Tyler's afraid of the dark."

"I'm not afraid of it. I just like to see what's happening."

He laughed and let go of me, taking me by the hand. "Just follow me," he said.

He led me through the crowd of people, and I heard him open a door. Then he pulled me through, shut the door and turned on the lights. We were in the other half of the basement. It had a washer and dryer at one end and an enormous pool table next to where we were standing.

"Do you know how to play pool, Billy?"

"Forget it, Tobey."

"Forget what?"

"I'm not going to teach you. Wynn's father would kill me if you scratched the table."

He sat down on the edge of the pool table, which made him almost the same height as me, then pulled me over in front of him. "Put your arms around my neck, Tobey."

"What for?"

"Because I'm going to kiss you."

"What if I don't want you to?"

"Then you walk back out that door."

I was trying to decide whether I'd rather kiss Billy or go back in the dark where all those other people were kissing, when he took my arms and put them around his neck himself.

"When are you going to quit fighting me, Tobey," he said right before his mouth closed over mine. Fireworks didn't go off, and the earth didn't move. It was more like being sacked and having twelve guys pile on top of me. In other words, his kiss took my breath away. And then, for no reason, he just stopped.

I flashed him a look of annoyance. "What did you stop for?"

He looked amused. "Tobey, you're supposed to at least move your lips a little when someone's kissing you."

"Nobody ever told me that."

"Well, I'm telling you."

And then he started kissing me again, and I moved my lips like he was moving his, and it was even better that way. And it went on for a lot more than ten seconds. In fact, I finally stopped counting and even closed my eyes, and it was two thousand times better than kissing Wynn or Charles. In fact, it was better than anything, except maybe making a touchdown. And then I stopped comparing it and just enjoyed it.

He finally decided he needed to breathe, I guess, and he just put his face next to mine and held me close. But pretty soon I figured he'd had enough time to catch up on his breathing, and I moved my head so that our mouths were touching again and we started in again kissing. It was a very nice feeling, like I was wrapped in this warm cocoon and nothing bad could ever happen to me. Oh no, it was even better than that, but I don't know how to describe it.

Finally he pulled away from me and just sat there staring at me. He had this really serious look, and Billy never looks serious about anything.

"You know what really bothers me, Billy Rafferty?" I asked him.

"What bothers you, Tobey Tyler?"

"I just don't understand how I can enjoy kissing the one boy in the whole world I truly hate."

"Let's not question that, Tobey," he said, leaning down towards me again.

I moved back. "No, I'm not kidding. It worries me."

"Maybe you should examine your premise."

"What does that mean?"

"It means maybe you don't really hate me."

I stood there shaking my head. "I don't understand anything anymore. I thought I hated you, and I thought I liked Wynn, but when he kissed me I didn't even feel anything, and with you . . ."

"Yes?"

"Never mind."

"So Wynn kissed you, huh?"

"Just once for ten seconds. And then I made Charles kiss me so that I could compare it with Wynn's."

"And how did it compare?"

I shrugged. "I didn't really like either of them."

"That's reassuring to hear."

I stood back from him and crossed my arms over my chest. "Does this mean I'm your girlfriend now?"

He laughed. "No, it just means that we've kissed."

"I'm not your girlfriend?"

"Do you want to be?"

"No, that would be too embarrassing. No one would even believe it. Everyone thinks we hate each other, Billy."

"Do you really care what people think?"

"Not usually," I admitted.

"Well, don't worry about it. You're too young to be my girlfriend."

"I am not!"

He laughed. "You'd wear me out. You'd want me to teach you pool and pole vaulting and whatever else you took a fancy to."

"But that would be fun."

"We're too much alike."

"That's what Charles said."

"Why are you giving me a hard time, Tobey?

was beginning to see that Billy was going to be a good friend, too, along with being my boyfriend. It would take up a whole lot of time just for him to teach me all the things I wanted to learn. Which reminded me.

"Will you teach me how to drive, Billy?"

"I was wondering when you'd get around to that."

"Well, someone's got to teach me."

"Yeah, I'll teach you, but not tonight."

"You remember that time you kept me prisoner in the empty house?"

"What made you think of that?"

"I don't know."

"Yeah, I remember."

I had been in the fifth grade at the time, and he had been in the sixth. There was this new house in the neighborhood that had just been built, but no one had moved in it yet. We had found an open window to the basement and had sneaked in it and used it for a secret hideout.

Up until that year I had always been about the same size as Billy, but suddenly he had started growing and that summer he was not only larger, but also stronger. We used to fight over everything in those days, too, but for some reason, on this particular day we sneaked in the house he got it into his head that I was going to have to kiss him or he wouldn't let me back out.

When we sneaked in, it was right after lunch, and when he told me I couldn't leave until I kissed him, I told him in that case I'd just stay there forever, because that was how long it was going to take before I'd ever kiss him.

He was just as stubborn as I was, so all day long we had played tic-tac-toe on the dusty floorboards, he too stubborn to give up his threat and me too stubborn to go along with it. The only way I ever got out of there was because finally it was dinner time and we both had to go home.

"You were so stubborn," I reminded him.

"Oh, I don't know, Tobey. If you had just kissed me then, maybe we wouldn't have wasted all this time."

"I would never have liked you then."

"I bet you were saying the same thing yesterday."

Well, there was some truth in that. In fact I couldn't figure out how I'd break the news to my mother. I wished now I hadn't been knocking Billy so much at home. But who would ever have thought I'd end up being his girlfriend?

He pulled up in front of my house and turned off the motor and the headlights. It was still early, and all the lights in the house were on. I was glad I didn't wear lipstick, so it wouldn't get all smeared and I'd have to walk in the house and explain that to my father.

"It might not be as much fun not fighting anymore," I said.

"Who said we won't fight anymore?"

"Oh, good. I was afraid maybe you'd get mellow or something."

"Just when we're kissing. All the rest of the time I think we should fight."

I was about to agree with him, but then he turned my head and we were kissing again. It was just as exciting as fighting, in its own way. Then I started thinking about what our first fight would be about. Then I stopped thinking at all.

Then he pulled away and said, "You want me to call you in the morning and wake you up?"

I nodded happily.

"Goodnight, brat." I liked that. It sounded much better than "honey" or "darling."

I got out of the car. He waited until I got in the front door; then I waved to him as he drove off. I walked through the living room, and my mother said, "You're home pretty early. Wasn't the party any fun?"

"It was a great party," I told her. "And guess what? I have a boyfriend."

She smiled. "Billy Rafferty?"

"How did you know?"

"I have eyes."

How could she possibly have known when *I* didn't even know. I went into the kitchen and got an apple, then went upstairs to my room. About a minute later Robin came in.

"Wasn't that Billy Rafferty who brought you home?"

"Yes, it was."

"I saw you kissing him in his car!"

"So?"

"I thought you hated Billy Rafferty."

"Sometimes, Robin, the first indication that you like someone is when you hate him."

She digested that for a moment, then, "Is that the truth?"

"I just told you, didn't I?"

She nodded.

It's always good to share your knowledge with the young.

Four exciting First Love from Silhouette romances yours for 15 days—_free!_

If you enjoyed this First Love from Silhouette,® you'll want to read more! These are true-to-life romances about the things that matter most to you now—your friendships, dating, getting along in school, and learning about yourself. The stories could really happen, and the characters are so real they'll seem like friends.

Now you can get 4 First Love from Silhouette romances to look over for 15 days—absolutely free! If you decide not to keep them, simply return them and pay nothing. But if you enjoy them as much as we believe you will, keep them and pay the invoice enclosed with your trial shipment. You'll then become a member of the First Love from Silhouette℠ Book Club and will receive 4 more new First Love from Silhouette romances every month. You'll always be among the first to get them, and you'll never miss a new title. There is no minimum number of books to buy and you can cancel at any time. To receive your 4 books, mail the coupon below today.

First Love from Silhouette® is a service mark and a registered trademark of Simon & Schuster

First Love from Silhouette

THERE'S NOTHING QUITE AS SPECIAL AS A FIRST LOVE.

--- **$1.75 each** ---

2 □ GIRL IN THE ROUGH Wunsch

3 □ PLEASE LET ME IN Beckman

4 □ SERENADE Marceau

6 □ KATE HERSELF Erskine

7 □ SONGBIRD Enfield

14 □ PROMISED KISS Ladd

15 □ SUMMER ROMANCE Diamond

16 □ SOMEONE TO LOVE Bryan

17 □ GOLDEN GIRL Erskine

18 □ WE BELONG TOGETHER Harper

19 □ TOMORROW'S WISH Ryan

20 □ SAY PLEASE! Francis

--- **$1.95** ---

24 □ DREAM LOVER Treadwell

26 □ A TIME FOR US Ryan

27 □ A SECRET PLACE Francis

29 □ FOR THE LOVE OF LORI Ladd

30 □ A BOY TO DREAM ABOUT Quinn

31 □ THE FIRST ACT London

32 □ DARE TO LOVE Bush

33 □ YOU AND ME Johnson

34 □ THE PERFECT FIGURE March

35 □ PEOPLE LIKE US Haynes

36 □ ONE ON ONE Ketter

37 □ LOVE NOTE Howell

38 □ ALL-AMERICAN GIRL Payton

39 □ BE MY VALENTINE Harper

40 □ MY LUCKY STAR Cassiday

41 □ JUST FRIENDS Francis

42 □ PROMISES TO COME Dellin

43 □ A KNIGHT TO REMEMBER Martin

44 □ SOMEONE LIKE JEREMY VAUGHN Alexander

45 □ A TOUCH OF LOVE Madison

46 □ SEALED WITH A KISS Davis

47 □ THREE WEEKS OF LOVE Aks

48 □ SUMMER ILLUSION Manning

49 □ ONE OF A KIND Brett

50 □ STAY, SWEET LOVE Fisher

51 □ PRAIRIE GIRL Coy

52 □ A SUMMER TO REMEMBER Robertson

First Love from Silhouette

- 53 ☐ LIGHT OF MY LIFE Harper
- 54 ☐ PICTURE PERFECT Enfield
- 55 ☐ LOVE ON THE RUN Graham
- 56 ☐ ROMANCE IN STORE Arthur
- 57 ☐ SOME DAY MY PRINCE Ladd
- 58 ☐ DOUBLE EXPOSURE Hawkins
- 59 ☐ A RAINBOW FOR ALISON Johnson
- 60 ☐ ALABAMA MOON Cole
- 61 ☐ HERE COMES KARY! Dunne

- 62 ☐ SECRET ADMIRER Enfield
- 63 ☐ A NEW BEGINNING Ryan
- 64 ☐ MIX AND MATCH Madison
- 65 ☐ THE MYSTERY KISS Harper
- 66 ☐ UP TO DATE Sommers
- 67 ☐ PUPPY LOVE Harrell
- 68 ☐ CHANGE PARTNERS Wagner
- 69 ☐ ADVICE AND CONSENT Alexander

- 70 ☐ MORE THAN FRIENDS Stuart
- 71 ☐ THAT CERTAIN BOY Malek
- 72 ☐ LOVE AND HONORS Ryan
- 73 ☐ SHORT STOP FOR ROMANCE Harper
- 74 ☐ A PASSING GAME Sommers
- 75 ☐ UNDER THE MISTLETOE Mathews
- 76 ☐ SEND IN THE CLOWNS Youngblood

FIRST LOVE, Department FL/4
1230 Avenue of the Americas
New York, NY 10020

Please send me the books I have checked above. I am enclosing
$_____ (please add 75¢ to cover postage and handling. NYS and
NYC residents please add appropriate sales tax). Send check
or money order—no cash or C.O.D.'s please. Allow six weeks for
delivery.

NAME _____

ADDRESS _____

CITY _____ STATE/ZIP _____

Genuine Silhouette sterling silver bookmark for only $15.95!

What a beautiful way to hold your place in your current romance! This genuine sterling silver bookmark, with the distinctive Silhouette symbol in elegant black, measures 1½" long and 1" wide. It makes a beautiful gift for yourself, and for every romantic you know! And, at only $15.95 each, including all postage and handling charges, you'll want to order several now, while supplies last.

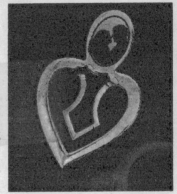

Send your name and address with check or money order for $15.95 per bookmark ordered to
Simon & Schuster Enterprises
120 Brighton Rd., P.O. Box 5020
Clifton, N.J. 07012
Attn: Bookmark

Bookmarks can be ordered pre-paid only. No charges will be accepted. Please allow 4-6 weeks for delivery.

N.Y. State Residents
Please Add Sales Tax